Henry's Promise

Henry's Promise

Marcel Laporte

ARPress
ILLUMINATING IDEAS
EMPOWERING VOICES

Copyright © 2022 by Marcel Laporte

All rights reserved. No part of this publication may be reproduced, distributed, or transmitted in any form or by any means, including photocopying, recording, or other electronic or mechanical methods, without the prior written permission of the copyright owner and the publisher, except in the case of brief quotations embodied in critical reviews and certain other noncommercial uses permitted by copyright law.For permission requests,write to the publisher, addressed "Attention: Permissions Coordinator," at the address below.

ARPress
45 Dan Road Suite 5
Canton, MA 02021

Hotline: 1(888) 821-0229
Fax: 1(508) 545-7580

Ordering Information:
Quantity sales. Special discounts are available on quantity purchases by corporations,associations, and others. For details, contact the publisher at the address above.

Printed in the United States of America.

ISBN-13:   Softcover   979-8-89330-717-7
                     eBook   979-8-89330-718-4

Library of Congress Control Number: 2024901866

TABLE OF CONTENS

FOREWORD

How often have we heard the words till death do us part? For couples it is only a line that needs to be said in the process of getting married. Over the years I attended my fair share of weddings, I like weddings, being part of the celebration of a new chapter in life for the bride and groom. One thing that I noticed when the bride and groom are exchanging personal vows, the words till death do us part or for that matter no words are mentioned being together until the grim reaper comes knocking at your door. You can always hear the words " I am marrying my best friend", I will be faithful, etc....... But no words stating that they will be together until the end of their days. What you are about to read in this book is fictional. A story about devotion, the meaning of true love and keeping the promise till death do us part. But I wonder if some couples will go the distance when it comes to sickness and in health and hang on until the end. I have witnessed to many breakups because of health issues in couples' lives. When someone says, " I love you to death, you captured my heart, I will always love you". Do they really know the meaning of the words? This book is based on a fictional character named Henry no matter the obstacles and hardship, he will do everything in his power to keep the promise of the famous words till death do us part.

CHAPTER 1

Henry was seven years old and his sister Louane eleven years old when their parents were killed in a car crash. Henry was only two years old when his parents decided to pack up and move from South Africa to the United States.

His dad was under the assumption, convinced they could live a life of luxury without much effort on his part, the land of opportunities and all that jazz. Before moving to the "U.S" Henry's dad "Raoul" was struggling to make ends meet.

He was only fifteen years old when he dropped out of high school. His dream like so many of us was to make a lot of money and no patience to wait until he graduated from high school. Fame and fortune were waiting for him.

His motto was I can read and write that is all I need and when I find a job I like with a good salary, I will learn as I go on the job training. I will not have any problems because I am a fast learner.

The sad part by not finishing high school, he could only find minimum wage jobs. His parents urged him to go back to school. He refused stating that his dream job was just around the corner but which corner? He met his future wife "Corrina" at a friend's birthday party. They were both nineteen years old. Six months into the relationship Corrina was pregnant.

" Guess what honey I am pregnant." he replied

" We cannot afford to have a baby."

" I know that you do not make a lot of money, but it does not eliminate the fact that I am pregnant. "

They eventually married with only their parents by their side. No money for a celebration with family and friends. Four months after the wedding Henry's older sister " Louane" was born his dad was still only making minimum wage.

They were really struggling to put food on the table. His wife could not find work. She was also a high school dropout. One day when he came home from work, she gave him the news that she was pregnant.

" Not again"

" Yes, again the doctor confirmed today I am in my second month of pregnancy."

When Henry was born his dad was working two jobs. After is shift washing dishes at a local restaurant, he would go to his second job at a junkyard. He was working fourteen hours a day. Six days a week. One day when he came home from work, he said to his wife Corrina

" We are moving to America"

" We are moving where?"

" To America"

" To America really to America"

" that's right America"

" Why America? What made you think to move to America?"

" One of my coworkers at the junkyard is moving to America, he said it is a land of opportunity, you can have a high paying job, make good money without much education. A life of luxury, live in big houses with nice furniture, nice cars, fancy clothes, the whole nine yards and even more."

" I am curious to know how your coworker friend is so sure to get a high paying job when he moves to the states."

" His brother lives in the states and told him if he moved to the "U.S" he will have a job waiting for him. His brother owns a trucking company."

" Ok but is not the same if we move to the states, you will not have a job waiting for you and where in the states are we going to move to."

When Henry's dad was finally able to convince his mom to move, he decided to move to the state of California where it is always warm and as per his dad better paying jobs.

They packed their belongings and used his final paycheck to cover the cost to move to the "U.S" they settled in a city called Sacramento California once in the "U.S" life was not easy for Henry's family, they had no money. They lived in homeless shelters. Henry's sister rebelled she did not want to leave her home in South Africa.

It took his dad a few months before he was able to find work, again as a dishwasher for a local restaurant. They moved into a small apartment situated in a low rent housing complex with a high crime rate. Henry shared his bedroom with his rebellious sister. His mom and dad would argue about money. They relied on a food bank for food and hand me down clothes.

After a few months of washing dishes his dad was able to get a job as a janitor at a local high school again a minimum wage job. Henry's dad finally realized it was a mistake to move and the land of opportunity is not all what he expected.

When Henry started grade school his mother was able to find a part time job cleaning houses, with the extra money they were able to buy an old car, barely legal to be on the road. Henry was short for his age, being the shortest kid in his class, the hand me down clothes he was wearing and especially his weird accent made him a target for every bully in school.

He was beaten almost every day; the other kids would laugh at him. Each day at school he would hear a new slogan aimed at him. Louane was lucky it did not take her long to make new friends. At school Louane did not bother to look after her little brother

" Hey guys look at what short stuff is wearing today, where did you get your clothes? I know when rummaging in trash cans again. "

" Half pint are you going to cry again today? "

" The little midget stinks, he does not have any friends"

" What a ridiculous and stupid family name like (Engelbrecht). "

He was pushed in puddles of water, kicked, and punched. His mom talked with the school's principal if there was something he could do. He did very little next to nothing to rectify the issue. The teasing and getting beaten continued until a new kid in school named Lucas stood up for him.

" Leave him alone he does not bother anybody." the bullies were talking among themselves.

" Who is he? "

" He is a new student named Lucas. He started attending our school last week." one of the bullies shouted at Lucas

" Hey, you do not waste your time with that loser, come and join us. "Lucas walked over to the bully who was yelling at him to join them.

" He is not a loser because I am looking at the loser including his friends. Does it make you feel good to tease him? Teasing him does not say much for you. You need to put someone down to make yourself look good. It is not his fault for the way he looks. "

The bully was now red in the face because of being put on the spot. His friends not saying a word.

" His parents are poor and being a little shorter than everybody else is no excuse to laugh at him. Do that again and you will have to deal with me. Do you have anything else to say. Fatso."

Fatso and his buddies walked away, a few of his friends were laughing

" Fatso that's funny."

Lucas watched the bullies walk away; Lucas made is way over where Henry was standing.

" Thank you but I do not know you, why did you defend me? "

" My name is Lucas we moved down the same street where you live, the first house on your left when you leave the low renting housing units. My dad's name is Steve and my mom's name is Lisa my family name is Moore."

Lucas was eight years old a year older than Henry, his dad worked in the electronics industry his mom was a chef. His dad was transferred from the company's head office located in Chicago to take a job as a supervisor in the manufacturing division for the electronics company.

Lucas was a year older than everybody else in his class, in grade school he needed to repeat the second grade.

" My name is Henry thank you again for standing up for me. Every day they push me, call me names. I am scared to go to school because I know the gang will be there waiting for me. My mom talked to the school's principle; it did not change anything I do not have any friends."

" Well, you have one now, at my old school it was the same thing bullies picking on the kids they knew would not defend themselves. Do you have any brothers or sisters?"

" One sister her name is Louane."

" I have two older sisters Julie is ten years old and Nicole twelve years old, they are not always nice with me. They are always picking on me. Come on let's go home."

While walking home they exchanged information

" Where are you from Henry? "

" I have been living in America now for five years, I was only two years old when my dad decided to come to America, I am originally from South Africa,"

" But you are white, I thought only black people live in Africa? "

" No also lots of people from South Africa are white, the village where I used to live, my dad told me most people are white like me. You look strong Lucas maybe that's why the bullies did not do anything when you talked to them, I think they were scared of you."

Lucas was tall for his age. It did not take long for Lucas and Henry to become best friends; they were like brothers. When Henry's parents died in a car crash, Henry was devastated, his sister did not show any emotions. When his mom and dad died Henry and his sister were at school.

When they came home from school, the house was empty. His mom and dad should be back by now, they were out shopping for a new car. Several hours passed when a police officer knocked on the door.

When Henry answered the door, he started crying there was a police officer at the door. He was scared that he might have done something wrong for a police officer to come knocking at their door.

" Mr. officer my mom and dad are not home yet. "

" Who else is here with you? "

" My sister Louane."

Louane made her way to the door to see what was going on.

" Is there someone else in the house? "

" Just the two of us officer."

" Do you have any relatives living nearby? "

" No mister police officer, only me and Henry and my mom and dad."

" Stay right here I will be right back."

" Ok."

The police officer walked to his patrol car and called the station for someone to contact a social worker. The police officer rejoined Henry and his sister. When the social worker arrived, the police officer explained why she was at their home.

The police officer broke the news to Henry and his sister that their mom and dad would not be coming home. The social worker introduced herself helped Henry and his sister to pack a few things. They were brought to a shelter. They remained at the shelter until they could find foster parents for both. Henry said to his sister.

" Why are you not crying mom and dad are dead? "

" Crying is for whimps."

Child welfare placed Henry and his sister in different foster homes. Henry wanted to stay in the same house with his sister, sadly it was not possible due to the lack of foster parents willing to take two foster children.

Henry had a hard time to adjust living with strangers, he would cry himself to sleep every night. Luca's parents went to the child welfare office to start the process to bring Henry and his sister to live with them.

When the application was finally approved Henry was ecstatic, but his sister wanted to stay put where she was. Child welfare decided that Henry's sister could stay with her foster parents. When Henry moved to his new home, first thing on the agenda was to bring Henry shopping for new clothes and getting a haircut.

The first day at school with the new clothes Henry was wearing, a haircut. Everybody was looking at him even the bullies that used to pick on him, where looking. It took about a minute for the kids in the schoolyard to gather around in circles, you could hear the chit chat.

Lucas was alongside Henry and spoke

" They are still looking, they are in circles talking about you, they must be wondering where the new clothes come from."

In high school they were named tall and short. They were also nicknamed twins like the movie with Danny DeVito and Arnold Schwarzenegger. In high school, Lucas was very athletic he played football, basketball, and baseball. Lucas was good looking, and many schoolgirls had a crush on him. When they graduated from high school Henry was only five foot five and Lucas was six feet tall.

After graduating from high school. Henry went to college to become a school teacher, Lucas joined the marines. For the first time since Henry moving in with Lucas family. The two friends won't be side by side anymore. Henry was not pleased with the fact that Lucas was joining the marines.

" Why the marines, why not go to college instead of the marines, are you aware that one day you might go into battle in a foreign country? We are like brothers; I cannot bear the thought of you getting hurt or even killed in battle. You know mom and dad are not too crazy about the idea of you joining the marines."

" I know they are not too crazy about the fact that I am enlisting in the army, my choice, my life. I know there are risks that comes with joining the army, but it is a career that I have chosen and Henry we are not like brothers, we are brothers whatever happens never forget that we are brothers. I am leaving for boot camp in a few months. I will come back when on leave or vacation, we will get together for drinks. "

Lucas and Henry spent one last summer together before the walk of life sends them in different directions.

" I am leaving for college in a week, please be careful I do not want to lose my brother."

The day came for Henry to leave for college, Henry and Lucas were both crying when they said their goodbyes. The college Henry attended was a four-hour drive from home. Two days later, Lucas left for boot camp.

Over the years Henry lost track of his sister Louane, apparently, she moved back to South Africa. Henry rented a small apartment near the college. While in college Henry held a part time job at a gas station, to help pay for his education.

CHAPTER 2

Henry worked hard in college keeping a part time job and studying for exams. Luca's parents paid a good portion of his expenses. In college Henry did not make too many friends, he kept to himself, he focused more on getting good grades and come graduation day. He will be a certified teacher.

His hard work paid off, after graduation he landed a teaching job in his home town, the same school that the bullies were always picking on him, until the day Lucas intervened and came to his rescue. He said to himself

" What a sweet reward to be able to teach at this school, if only the bullies could see me now."

After a year of teaching at his old school, Henry saw an ad on the internet. A high school in San Diego was looking for teachers, with better pay and benefits, he decided to apply for one of the jobs. He flew to San Diego for an interview and flew back home.

A week of anxious waiting went by. The phone rang the school board representative at the other end of the line gave Henry the good news, he got the job. He was given a month to prepare and move to San Diego

Henry will be teaching grade 10 math. He advised his employer; he would be leaving his teaching position in two weeks. His boss was sorry to see him go but understood. His fellow teachers organized a little farewell party for Henry, he said his goodbyes.

Everybody wished him luck. He was happy to move to San Diego. It would be a new adventure for someone coming from a midsize town. A bright future was ahead for him. He was able to find a nice apartment only one block away from the school where he will be teaching. He would meet his future wife in a very short time, that will forever change his life.

Henry's future wife is named Kaccha she was in the states with a student visa, she was studying chemistry at the San Diego university, so she could work in a lab back home. Kaccha was from India and planned to go back home the following day after her graduation.

Her parents were paying for her stay in the U.S and university fees. Her parents wanted her back home asap. Like Henry, Kaccha did not focus on making friends. Her main focus was her studies, graduating and going back home. When graduation was only days away her dad sent her some money to buy a plane ticket to go home. As faith would have it, she would not be going home.

After a day of celebrations and receiving her well-deserved diploma in hand, Kaccha was walking home, she was excited and looking forward to going back home, it was night time and the street where she lived was dark with only a few street lights.

At first, she did not notice the two men following her, as they were getting closer and closer. Kaccha started to run with the two men giving chase. Kaccha tripped and fell in a gully and landed in two feet of water.

The two men ran away in fear of getting caught by the cops. Kaccha was able to pull herself out of the water but could not go any further. She was crying and yelling for help.

Ironically Henry was going home after doing some shopping when he decided to take a shortcut home which brought him to the same dark street that Kaccha took to go home, when she was chased by the two men and fell in the gully. Instead of taking the car to go to work, Henry walked twenty minutes to work to stay in shape.

Henry was walking near the gully; he heard a faint cry for help. He stopped walking for a moment, he could not hear anything, as he was about to start walking again, he heard a faint voice crying for help.

" Hello anybody there? "

" Please help me I am down here, I tripped and fell in the gully, I am hurt, and I need help. Please help me."

" Hold on I am coming down "

" Please hurry I am cold I have been down here for over an hour."

When Henry finally reached her, he realized that he would not be able to pull Kaccha from the gully to the street by himself. He would need help. He covered her with his jacket and said.

" I am going to get help."

" No please a man who said he was going to help me said he was going for help and never came back."

" I will not be able to bring you back up the hill by myself. I will need help just hang on I will go for help and be back as soon as possible."

" Please sir do not leave me down here please "

" I promise I will call 911 and I will come back."

" Please hurry I do not like to be alone down here."

Henry could not get a signal on his cellphone he needed to climb back on the street to make the call.

" I do not have any money for an ambulance "

" Let me worry about that, I will only be a few minutes and I will comeback"

Henry climbed the hill and called 911.

" 911 what is your emergency. "

" A lady fell in a gully, and she is hurt, we need an ambulance asap, we are at the very end of Esther Street behind building number 42. Please hurry she has been down there for over an hour; she is cold and hurt. "

" Ok sir I have dispatched an ambulance, the fire department, and the police, please stay on the side of the road until help arrives, someone should be there in a few minutes ok, like I said stay put you will be able to guide the first responders to the location of the lady in distress. "

" Ok "

" Is the lady in question still conscious? "

" Just a moment please. Help will be here soon, I am not going anywhere, I have to stay up here until help arrives. "

" Thank you but I do not have any money for an ambulance."

" Let me worry about that, you will be safe and sound in a few minutes ok just hang on I can hear the sirens they will be here in a minute."

" Ok then you can hear the sirens I will end the call. "

" Thank you. "

When the first responders arrived, Henry said

" Follow me "

The first responders followed Henry down the hill, when they reached Kaccha she was unconscious, one of the first responder's said

" I have a few questions for you."

" Was she unconscious when you found her. Because 911 said she was responsive.? "

" No but she said she was cold that's why I covered her with my jacket and called you guys and she was responsive a few minutes ago. "

" Do you know her? "

" No, I was walking home when I heard her cries for help."

The first responders were able to put Kaccha on a stretcher in a matter of minutes, climb the hill and into the ambulance, by that time Kaccha regained consciousness

" I do not want to be in this ambulance, I am ok I want to go home, I have no money."

First responder.

" ma'am we need to get you to a hospital; you have injuries, and you are also suffering from hyperthermia."

" No, you do not understand I am supposed to go home tomorrow, my parents will be waiting for me."

" Sorry ma'am like I said we need to bring you to the hospital."

Henry seated himself beside her in the ambulance, took her hand.

" Do not worry, I am the one who found you in the gully, I will go with you to the hospital."

" But why are you doing this? I do not know you."

" My name is Henry and why am I helping you? In grade school I have a friend who at the time was a stranger to me, he stood up for me when the school bullies would not leave me alone. I learned a valuable lesson from him, you do not need to know the individual in order to help someone. So, relax everything will be fine."

The ambulance was now on its way to the hospital.

" You do not understand I am going back home to India tomorrow; I cannot miss my flight."

" We will worry about your flight later; the number one priority right now is to get you to the hospital and see a doctor. What happened did someone push you? "

" No, I was chased by two men. Do you think I will still be able to go home tomorrow.? If I do not go back tomorrow if I have to wait a few days before catching the next plane to go home, I have no place to stay, my rent is paid until tomorrow, that's why I need to go home."

" The police is following us."

" No please no police stop the ambulance so I can go home please."

" Like I said your first option is for you to get better so that you can go home to your family "

When the ambulance arrived at the hospital, the emergency room doctor was waiting for her. When the doctor was done with his examination, he advised Kaccha due to her injuries she will need to stay at the hospital for several days. The police officers were waiting to question Kaccha.

" Doctor, can we ask the young lady some questions.?

" No doctor I cannot stay you do not understand I have no money and I am supposed to go home tomorrow."

" I am sorry miss, but you need to stay in the hospital for a few days, if I release you from the hospital today, you will not feel well enough to go home, understood."

The doctor and the police officer turned to Henry.

" How long have you known her is she always this stubborn.? "

" No officer I am the one who heard her cries for help and called 911. Before tonight I have never seen this woman before."

" Why are you here then.? "

" She was hurt and scared, I told her that I would not leave her side until I was sure that she would be ok."

The officer turned his attention to Kaccha

" Miss I am officer drake; I need to ask you a few questions.?

" I do not know anything or anybody, I was walking home two men chased me and I fell in the gully. Can you tell the doctor for me please to release me from the hospital.? I need to go home to India tomorrow."

" Sorry miss I cannot do that, that's a decision the doctor will have to make. Were you able to see or hear the men that were chasing you.?

" No, I did not see their faces, it was dark. Both men were wearing black clothing. They ran away when I tripped and fell in the water. That is all I know. Now please can you leave me alone so that I can talk to the doctor? "

" Ok miss we will be in touch if we need to talk to you again."

On his way out the cop stopped to talk to Henry.

" You committed yourself to her she might not want you to leave. She attached herself to you because she is alone in this country and you are the person that was nice enough to help her in her time of need, for a lady that comes from India she speaks pretty good English. Did you see anything out of the ordinary when you heard her cries for help.? "

" No nothing at all."

" Thank you here is my card in case you need to contact me, have a good night."

" Good night."

Kaccha spotted Henry talking to the doctor.

" Please Harry help me to try to understand what is going on please, I do not understand."

The doctor gave Kaccha a sedative for her to calm down and eventually fall asleep.

" What is that something to put me to sleep, I do not want to sleep I cannot pay for anything."

" No need to worry about money this is a community hospital for the people who do not have any insurance or no money for medical treatment."

Kaccha was looking at Henry

" But if I do fall asleep, will you be here when I wake up.? "

" Yes, I will stay for a little while."

She finally fell asleep. Henry enquired.

" Doctor, do you have an idea how long she will be asleep." not too long I hope my parents are coming for a visit? "

" Do not worry she will be awake in a few hours, she does not have any broken bones, a few bruises but nothing serious, she is also suffering from hyperthermia, several days in the hospital will do her some good. "

" I guess I have to be here when she wakes up, I promised her that I would be here."

" That you did, grab the chair in the corner, you might be here for a while, I will go check on other patients, I will be back in a few hours, nurse if there is a change in her condition, page me."

" I will doctor."

Henry tried to make himself as comfortable as possible, he fell asleep while waiting for Kaccha to wake up. When Kaccha woke up she saw Henry sleeping in the chair, the doctor walked into the room.

" Are you feeling a little better? We will transfer you to a room upstairs, the nurse will come and get you in a few minutes."

Henry woke up, still a little drowsy.

" What's going on.? "

" They will bring me upstairs in a room."

" Ok then everything seems to be under control, I will be on my way. Goodbye and good luck."

" You are leaving, you said you would stay with me until everything is ok."

" I am sorry, but with all due respect Kaccha I stayed until everything was ok, you are out of danger now. I need to go home and have dinner and get a good night sleep. My foster parents are coming tomorrow for a visit before they move back to Chicago. I am truly sorry, but I have to go."

Kaccha started crying,

" You said until I was ok to go back to my home, but you are leaving why? " In my culture when you make a promise you keep your promise no matter what."

Henry shook his head and started pacing the floor, thinking why should I stay, I did not know her until a few hours ago. She is old enough to fend for herself, what did I get myself into?

" You need to call my parents in India for me, explain what happened you will need to talk very slow; they do not understand English very well, not like me."

" Ok ok I will call them when I get home."

Henry decided to spend the night at the hospital sleeping in the chair next to Kaccha's bed. The chair was not very comfortable, so he asked a nurse if she could find him a more comfortable chair to spend the night, after a few minutes the nurse came back dragging a recliner behind her.

" Thank you, very much I really appreciate the fact that you took the time to find a chair for me, again thank you."

" Your welcome sir, have a goodnight. "

Henry settled in for the night. The next morning when he woke up, Kaccha was sitting in bed having breakfast.

" Good morning Harry, the doctor told me I needed to stay one more day in the hospital, until tomorrow and I can go home."

" Great news by the way my name is Henry not Harry. Now that I know that you're going to be fine I will be going home."

" Are you going to come back? Are you going to call my parents? Their number is in my coat pocket, do you know how to call different countries.? Do not talk long it will cost more money, you need to come to the hospital to tell me what my dad said, please."

" Ok I will call and come back to tell you what your parents said. "

" Ok thank you, I am so lucky that you are around to help me. Tell my father I tripped again I have very clumsy feet."

Henry said goodbye and told her he would be back later that day. He took a taxi home, once in the taxi he was trying to find a solution for his predicament. He said to himself,

" I need to find a solution and fast I have to go to work Monday morning."

First thing Henry did when he arrived home, he called his adoptive parents and told them about Kaccha and maybe they should cancel their visit. They were already on their way and almost at his place, wanting more information about the situation once they get to his place.

Henry took the piece of paper with Kaccha's parents phone number from his pocket and called to explain why Kaccha was not on the plane to go home. Kaccha's dad answered the phone in the Hindi language, thinking that it was his daughter calling.

Henry paused for a moment trying to find the right words to start the conversation, he realized that he did not even know Kaccha's family name, awkward, well here goes nothing.

" Good day sir, my name is Henry, and I am calling on behalf of your daughter Kaccha, she is in the hospital she was not able to take the plane home, she will be out of the hospital tomorrow."

" Hello who you are, why Kaccha not calling? "

" Ok sir my name is Henry a friend of Kaccha."

" Kaccha no friends, I call U.S. police."

" Sir Kaccha was on her way home, and she had a little accident, and she is now in the hospital."

" Kaccha in hospital, bad, no plane today. "

Kaccha's dad put the phone down to talk to his wife, picks up the phone again.

" Allo, Allo, in hospital hurt no home today, when? She need money, she no stay, no money. No hospital tomorrow, come home. What she falls again? "

" Yes, sir she will be leaving the hospital tomorrow."

" Stay where, she calls me when she no more hospital ok, you take care of Kaccha, you reward, ok kind sir."

Kumar ended the call; Henry was puzzled as to why he did not inquire about her injuries. I guess he wants her to tell him in their language.

Henry heard a knock on the door. Surprise, surprise, it was Lucas, they hugged, at the same moment, mom and dad arrived, tears of joy, hugs, they made their way in the house. Once settled in with drinks in hand, they made themselves comfortable in the living room, Henry said

" Boy what a surprise when I opened the door and saw your ugly mug."

" I know you were lost for words, happy to see me, you could not believe I was standing in the doorway."

" Ok it's enough smart ass, but I have to admit all of us sitting in the same room sure feels nice. Cheers everyone."

They raised their glasses

" Cheers."

Mr. Moore wanted to talk about what Henry told him on the phone.

" So, Henry tell me what happened and what is going on? "

Henry did not get a chance to answer before Lucas cut in the conversation

" Whoa guys what are you two talking about? "

" Sit down Lucas let me talk and explain the situation that I got myself into. "

Henry explained in great detail the dilemma he was in for helping another human being.

" She is expecting me to go back to the hospital tonight, I called her parents in India, I am not sure if her dad fully understood what I was trying to tell him."

" I will go with you to the hospital and see if there is something I can do to help, at what time do you need to be there? "

" Thank you, Lucas, for coming with me, I will go after dinner. When do you need to return to the army base.? "

" In five days, I took some time off to help mom and dad move back to Chicago, I took a little detour when they told me they were coming here for a visit."

" Dad how long are you planning to stay? "

" Well, the plan was to spend the night and leave in the morning, but we might stay an extra day to see how things go. Are you planning on spending the night and bring her home tomorrow when she is released from the hospital? "

" I hope I do not have to stay overnight; I have no idea what to do tomorrow. Mom what would you do if you were in my shoes? "

" Let me tell you this, because there is no one else to help her, she attached herself to you, right now you are her life line. My opinion you should not abandon her, bring her here tomorrow and then we can take it from there, come up with a solution. Ok now let's go to dinner I am starving."

They enjoyed a nice dinner, with Lisa being a chef, she was their food critic.

" Nice place but the food, well they tried. The sauce is note quite spicy enough and the chicken a little bit overcooked. "

When dinner was done, Henry was ready to go to the hospital and see how Kaccha was doing. Lucas tagged along. When they entered her room, she was sleeping. They made their way to the cafeteria to grab some coffee. They sat down at a table.

" Henry, have you noticed our beautiful she is? "

" No not really, with just a glance in the room you were able to see that she is beautiful. "

" Yes sir, take a good look at her you will know what I mean,"

After finishing their cup of coffee, they made their way back upstairs to Kaccha' s room.

" Remember what I said Henry take a good look at her you will see she is very attractive. Women from India are known to be very attractive. "

" Ok ok I will take a good look when we get back."

" I wonder if she has any sisters. "

" Come on Lucas this not the time and the place to try to find out that kind of information. Put your hormones on hold. "

When they entered the room, Kaccha was sitting on the side of the bed having dinner.

" Henry you are back; good I was getting a little worried not knowing if you would be back. Who is your friend? "

Lucas made is way towards the bed.

" I am Lucas, I am his best friend, we are like brothers, did Henry tell you how beautiful you are? "

She blushed and said

" No "

" My friend and so-called brother is in the military, he is on leave for five days. "

Henry took a good look at Kaccha and said to himself

" She really is beautiful how could I have not seen how beautiful she is until now? "

" Henry did you call my parents. "

" Yes, I talked to your dad, but I am not sure if he understood everything I said. He wants you to call him tomorrow. "

" When I get out of the hospital tomorrow, I have no place to go."

Lucas put his hand on Henry 's shoulder and motioned his head towards Kaccha.

" Tomorrow you can come at my place so you will be able to call your dad."

" Thank you Henry you are so sweet, my dad will be pleased with you for helping me. He might want to give you a reward, are you staying here with me tonight.? I hope so I feel safe when you are with me, I trust you, I feel close to you, will I be able to wear the same clothes that I was wearing the other night? "

" If you want me to stay, I will stay, yesterday I talked to the staff manager and told him about your predicament and if they could wash your clothes. Your clothes will be nice and clean when you leave the hospital."

" Thank you is your friend going to stay also, your friend is very handsome."

" Thank you, you are also a very beautiful women, no I will not stay the night, I will go back to Henry's place, my parents are visiting and leaving tomorrow, I want to spend some leisure time with them before we leave."

" That's nice to have your parents so close to you, my parents are in India which I hope to see them soon."

Lucas stayed for a couple hours and went home to join his parents.

" Nice to have met you Kaccha, take care, you never know our paths may cross again."

Lucas winked at Henry.

" Thank you Henry to spend the night with me but what about tomorrow when I leave the hospital.? "

" When it is time to leave the hospital, I will bring you to my home so you can call your dad."

" Sorry you already told me that. "

Lucas explained to his parents that Henry was spending the night, tomorrow when Kaccha is released from the hospital he will bring her home.

" Henry I am tired now I want to sleep; promise you will be here when I wake up."

" Do not worry I will be here in this chair waiting for you to wake up."

" You are so sweet; I am lucky that you are the one that came to my rescue. Good night Henry."

" Good night Kaccha."

When the nurse checked on Kaccha she noticed Henry was still by her bedside.

" Spending the night again. She is lucky to have you helping her, from what I can see she is getting attached to you. You never know situations like this one might lead to."

" I know where you are going with this, I do not think so, when she is released from the hospital tomorrow, I will bring her home so she can call her dad to make arrangements for her to go home, end of story."

" I am not so sure about that; anyway, good night my shift is over I am going home. If she needs help in the middle of the night do not hesitate to press this button. Well good night. "

" Goodnight, thank you for the good service."

" You're welcome. "

 the following morning when Kaccha woke up she was anxious to leave the hospital and go call her parents.

" Henry, Henry wake up, I want to leave now, what time is it? "

" Wha, Wha, what is going on to wake me up in such a hurry? "

" I want to leave the hospital now."

" Sorry my dear you cannot leave until the doctor comes to see you one last time before you are discharged from the hospital."

" Is he going to come soon to see me? "

" It is only eight thirty in the morning. "

The nurse entered the room to check on Kaccha and to tell her the doctor would probably see her around ten am. When the nurse was leaving the room a nurse's aide brought Kaccha her breakfast.

" Thank you but you did not bring any breakfast for my friend how come? "

"It's alright I will go to the cafeteria and get some breakfast, I will be back in about a half hour. "

On the way to the cafeteria Henry was wondering what to do when he brings Kaccha home. She will call her parents and then what? I guess I have to wait and see. When Henry returned from breakfast Kaccha was fully dressed and ready to leave the hospital.

" You were right Henry my clothes are clean and smell great, the doctor came a little early to tell me I can go home. I am sorry for my English I still have a lot to learn. "

" No worries you speak very good English."

" What do you mean no worries, does my way of talking worry you? "

" No no not at all it means everything is ok. "

" Ok, shall we go now, is your house far from here? I feel protected Henry when you are with me. "

Both Henry and Kaccha thanked the hospital staff for doing such a great job, took the elevator walked to his car. Henry opened the door for her and made is way to the driver's side. Started the car and on his way home with Kaccha.

" My house is about twenty minutes from here. Lucas and my parents are still at my place, you will be able to meet the parents that took me in when my mom and dad died in a car accident."

" So sorry for your parents, it is ok that I go to your house while they are still there? "

" Of course, it is ok, they are very good people, I was only eight years old when my parents died, I have an older sister that moved back to South Africa."

" You were born in South Africa that explains the nice accent when you talk."

When they arrived, everyone greeted Kaccha and made her feel like she was part of the family.

" I am blessed that Henry saved me that night and I get to meet you good people, not everyone would be lucky like me when they need help. Can I please go into your room to call my parents?

" Yes of course "

Henry handed her the phone, and she made her way to Henry's room, closed the door. They could hear her talk but did not understand a word she was talking to her dad in Arabic.

" I told you dad she was beautiful; Henry was trying to make me believe he had not noticed how beautiful she is. "

When she came out of the bedroom, they were all anxious to hear about her conversation with her dad.

" My dad say thank you very much he wanted to know if I could stay here for a few days because he will fly from India to meet you, then we fly back home. He said it was ok for me to wait for him here. He will be here in three days. Is it ok I hope?"

" Yes, you can wait for your dad here, no problem."

 Mr. Moore responded by saying.

" We all agree that everything is under control, we will get going in a few hours. "

" Dad I will stay a few more days in case Henry needs help."

" What kind of help do you think he will need, you want to stay here because of the girl, you said you took some time off to help with the move so when we leave your coming with us."

" Henry, are you going to share your bed with her? "

" Never mind you."

" Come on Henry it was just a little innocent question."

" Sure, it was."

A few hours later Mr. Moore and company were on their way to Chicago, leaving Henry alone with Kaccha.

CHAPTER 3

Kaccha was happy to be able to stay with Henry for the next three or four days until her dad arrives.

" Henry, I need to go to my place where I live to get my stuff, do you think you can drive me there please? "

" Yes, do you want to go now? "

" Yes please."

" The doctor advised you to stay home and get some rest. "

" I know but I have to go get my stuff. "

" Can it wait until tomorrow? "

" No please I want to go today. "

" Alrighty then let's go. Do you have a lot of stuff.? Maybe I should rent a truck? "

" No not much stuff, a few suitcases."

" What is the address.? "

" 2167 Dempster Street room number 4. "

When they arrived Kaccha was anxious to get her luggage, when she tried to unlock the door, her key would not fit in the keyhole.

" That is strange my key does not unlock my door anymore. "

" I have a pretty good idea why your key does not fit anymore; the owner of the place changed the lock. "

" Why would he do that, do you think my suitcases are still in my room? "

" Let's go find out, does the owner live in the building? "

" Yes, in the basement. "

They made their way to the basement and knocked on the door.

" Who is it? "

" Kaccha, I come to get my stuff."

The owner opened the door and let them in.

" What is the matter with you showing up a couple of days late to get your stuff? When you did not come back to get your stuff, I changed the lock on your door. Before I give you your suitcases you need to pay for the new lock and two days of storage fees."

" But you do not understand I was in the hospital for two days, that is why I was not able to get my suitcases and give you the key. "

" Am I supposed to believe that, when you left for school the other day, you looked healthy to me. Who is this your boyfriend? "

" Look sir my name is Henry, on her way home the other night she was chased by two men trying to outrun them she fell in a gully, I am the one who found her and called 911. She was released from the hospital this morning, so there was no way she could come and get her stuff until today. Did you rent her room to a new tenant? "

" No, where do you come from with that accent? I know at the end of a rainbow., with your height and accent it makes sense that you come from the end of a rainbow. "

" Very funny, it does not matter where I come from, you did not waste any time to change the lock on the door. "

" That is none of your business nowadays you cannot trust anyone that is why I changed the lock and brought her stuff down here."

" I cannot understand your way of thinking. Did you really think that she was going to leave the country without her luggage? "

" Here is your key, can I have my suitcases please? "

" Not until you pay for the lock and two days of storage."

" Two days of storage for what?"

" I was responsible for her luggage."

" How much money do I owe you, I have no money?

" Listen sir she gave you her key, now please go get the suitcases so that we can be on our way. She does not have to pay for the lock, I am sure you will use it again. "

" It is not my fault she spent a few days in the hospital, pay up or get out."

" Come on now she is going back home in a few days, she needs her stuff. How much for the lock? "

" Thirty-five bucks plus twenty dollars for storing her luggage."

" Here is your lousy fifty-five dollars."

" Thank you I will be right back."

Henry was thinking what a moron when the landlord came back with the suitcases.

" There you go, Mr. leprechaun, it was a pleasure doing business with you, now get off my property. I am sure she will find a way to pay you back if you know what I mean. Where she comes from that's how they pay their debts, they don't need any money they use their assets. "

Henry lunged and punched the guy in the face,

" You asshole."

" I am calling the cops."

Kaccha started crying,

" All I wanted was to get my stuff and now Henry is in trouble because of you."

" Get off my property now before I call the cops, you pack a good punch for a little guy, I guess I had it coming, now go, I never want to see both of you again."

Still fuming Henry brought the luggage to the car without saying a word.

" Henry why you do not talk to me, are you mad at me? "

" Of course not, you know this is the first time that I have punched someone, actually it felt good belting him one, what an asshole, while living there did he cause you any problems? "

" No, I would pay my rent and he would always say thank you, have a nice day. You know what Henry, nobody protected me before like you did. I feel sorry for you to have to punch him and get into trouble because of me. You are a good man Henry. I feel good with you, I like you a lot, is that ok? "

" Yes, it is ok, I feel the same way about you."

While driving home Kaccha smiled at Henry, took his hand.

" I have never felt like this for anyone, it is going to be hard to say goodbye. "

" Yes, I know me too. "

Henry parked the car in the driveway.

" We are home."

" Henry it is your home not mine, remember I am leaving in a few days."

" I know it is only a figure of speech to say we have arrived at our destination."

Henry put the suitcases in his room and closed the door

" Henry, you ok if I sleep in your room. I can sleep on couch."

" You are my guest and I want you to be comfortable." are you hungry?"

" Yes"

Henry cooked dinner and after dinner he cleared the table and did the dishes.

" I have to go to work tomorrow, will you be ok staying here alone keep the door locked. "

" Yes, I will be fine."

They spent the remainder of the evening getting to know each other, talked about family, friends when they were kids.

" My goodness look at the time, I think I will call it a day, I am pooped out. "

" Yes, I am tired, long day, goodnight."

She kissed Henry on the cheek and went to bed.

" Wake me tomorrow when you leave, I do not like to sleep in a new place alone."

" Ok see you in the morning, excuse me for a minute I need a pillow, blanket and clothes for the morning. "

Henry prepared his bed and laid down. In a matter of minutes Henry was sound asleep, Kaccha stood in the bedroom doorway for a few minutes, watching Henry sleep. She was starting to have feelings for him. She knew it will be difficult to say goodbye when she leaves to go back home. The next morning when Henry woke up Kaccha was sitting in the chair next to the couch.

" Good morning, Henry, did you sleep well? "

" Yes, what about you? "

" Not so much, I am worried what will happen when my dad is here and we go back home, I think I do not want to leave anymore, I want to stay here with you, I now love you Henry."

Kaccha with tears in her eyes, sat on the couch next to Henry and kissed him, Henry did not resist the kiss, he was happy because he felt the same way about her.

" I am happy you told me that you love me because I love you too. I have to get ready to go to work, feel right at home, plenty of food in the fridge."

Henry took a shower, when he was ready to leave for work, they hugged and kissed and Henry was off to work, Henry was sporting a big grin on his face, he finally knew what it was to fall in love. He could not wait for the day to end and go home to be with Kaccha. He was also worried about what will happen in a few days when her dad arrives to bring her back to India.

Some of his coworkers applauded him when he walked in, some curious to know what the story was, some did not care less. the ones wanting to know the details gathered around Henry. One of his colleagues said.

" So, mister hero we are all curious and waiting for you to tell us your story. "

" Boy give me a chance to at least put my lunch in the fridge, you guys are like a pack of hungry wolves. So anyway, do you guys pay someone to follow my every moves? "

" What do you mean have someone follow you? "

" Well, it's funny that everyone in this room is already aware about my adventures of Friday night."

Debbie a grade nine teacher said.

" My son-in-law is a paramedic and recognized you the other night."

" I was under the impression they are sworn to secrecy."

" They are, the only thing he said was that you were the one responsible to get her to a hospital, now talk we only have a little bit of time before classes start."

" I was walking home when I heard a cry for help, I stopped walking and listened, again I heard the cry for help. It turns out the young lady was being chased by two men when she tripped and fell down the gully. I reassured her that I was going to help her, I called 911 and the rest is history the paramedics took her away in an ambulance to the hospital."

" Yes, but you climbed in the ambulance with her. "

" Yes, I did she was scared, she did not want to be alone. "

" Where is she now? "

" At my place, before you ask why let me explain."

Henry filled them in all the details, where she was from, talked about her situation and her dad coming to the U.S to bring his daughter back home. One of the teachers said,

" For real you punched the guy in the face? "

" Yes, I did, and it felt good to clobber him."

" Good for you."

" When is her dad coming to bring her back home? "

" In a few days."

" Really do you know that you are responsible for her well-being until her dad arrives? "

" it's no big deal, she isn't any trouble."

" I think our friend Henry is falling in love."

" No, I am not, she is at my place because there is no place for her to go until her dad gets here. Now you all know as much as I do."

" I don't know Henry."

The school bell rang everybody scooted out the room to go join their students.

" Saved by the bell my dear Henry."

All day long between classes, lunch hour, they kept pressing poor Henry for more information, to no avail. The next morning at work, as soon as Henry walked in the door, he was inundated with questions, which was starting to irritate him, he was losing patience, he would reply nothing new.

When Henry came home from work, Kaccha was waiting for him with supper on the table. Henry was thinking he could get used to this. In the evening they would cuddle and talk until bedtime. They were now both madly in love.

" Henry my dad called this morning he will arrive at the airport tomorrow evening, can we go pick him up at the airport? "

" Of course."

" Henry, I have fallen in love with you, how can I tell my dad I do not want to leave anymore?"

" Very good question, I do not know how to answer that, I have no clue on how to break the news to him that you want to stay with me. The only thing that I can think of is when we arrive from the airport, no beating around the bush, we will tell him and hope that he will react with a positive attitude, he will agree that you stay. "

" What you mean beat the bush, I do not understand? "

" Sorry, what I mean is when we get to the house, we will tell him that you want to stay. "

" He is coming to get me and bring me home, he will be very mad at me for not wanting to go back, I am very nervous and scared for tomorrow when we speak to my father."

The following morning Henry's friends at work, could see a worried, nervous look on his face. One of his friends commented

" Tonight, is the night my friend."

" Yes, indeed tonight is the night."

By now Henry's friends knew about the love relationship between the two and the fear of meeting her dad.

" How is Kaccha coping with the thought she might have to leave with her dad, have you guys shared the bed yet? "

" God forbid no, it would be a sacrilege for her culture to say the least. I will not be at work tomorrow, I booked the day off, if I do not come back in a couple of days, that will mean that all hell broke loose, and I might end up in jail. I hope it does not come to that. For the first time in my life, except for Lucas and his family, I have someone to love and cherish, after tomorrow I might never see her again."

" I feel for you my friend I really do. "

" I know. "

When Henry came home after work, Kaccha advised him that her dad's flight was delayed by three hours, her mom was also coming. When the time came to go pick up her parents at the airport, Kaccha was very quiet. When they were only minutes away from the airport she said to Henry.

" I know Henry, we only have known each other for a week, but I feel that we should be together for the rest of our lives. I really do love you, Henry."

Henry reached over, grabbed her hand.

" I know exactly what you mean I feel the same way about you, like you said we've only known each other for a week, but when you know that you know it was meant to be, I might be repeating myself, but it was meant for me to be walking by when you needed help there is no way to deny that. I know we still have a lot the learn about each other, we will have ups and downs like everybody else, but we will navigate through the waves together hand in hand. We started our journey a week ago, if someone would have told me a few weeks ago that today I would be in love, I would have told he or she was crazy. Well, here we are, your dad's name is Kumar, your mom Suhani but how do you pronounce your family name again? "

" Krishenath ".

" I am sorry, I have a hard time with the pronunciation, especially with my South African accent, I do not want to insult your mom and dad. "

" It will be ok, my dad understands, our family name is hard to say. Krishenath. "

" Krishenath."

" Yes. Krishenath, I know my dad will also have problem with your family name. We are here, I have not seen my parents now for four months, I am excited and very worried at the same time. We are here."

Henry parked the car.

" Well here goes nothing is it ok if we hold hands? "

" Not now Henry, shall we go to see if they are here? "

They walked to the baggage claim area without saying a word, sat on a bench, after a few minutes of waiting Kaccha spotted her parents.

" They are here."

She ran towards them yelling

" Here I am "

They hugged and kissed. Henry stayed a few feet behind Kaccha until she introduced him to her parents.

" Mom, dad, my savior Henry. "

Her mom and dad embraced Henry with kisses. Her dad said.

" So, you Henry thank you, for helping my daughter and keep safe, I have a gift for you, for reward to help my daughter. My name is Kumar, and this is wife Suhani. "

" I am pleased to me you Mr. and Mrs. I apologize if I do not pronounce your name correctly Mr. and Mrs. Krishenath. "

" Very good yes Krishenath I am impressed did you practice my name? I think I have problem with your name Engelbrecht is that correct? "

" Close enough. "

" Thank you, Henry, where car? "

" Let me get your luggage and follow me. "

" I impressed polite young man."

They followed Henry to the car, Henry put the luggage in the trunk.

" I sit with you in front, Kaccha and mother in the back, ok? "

" Fine with me."

" Kaccha say you school teacher. "

" Yes, I am. "

" Hard job teacher, no make much money. Live far from airport? "

" No about twenty-five minutes."

" Twenty-five minutes far to drive to airport. "

" You must be hungry after such a long flight. "

" Yes, very hungry, almost twenty-four hours on plane, America far from India, good thing Kaccha coming home and no need to fly again, I am happy, Kaccha I speak to friend, he got job for you in laboratory not far from home good, yes? Kaccha, we leave tomorrow already have ticket for you, expensive to take plane. You need to tell me what happened yes but later we eat first. Go to restaurant or to your home to eat? "

" Do you want to go to a restaurant? "

" I like home, no restaurant wife Suhani cook good meal for us. I hope you no eat beef, cows sacred in India, if yes you stop now. Fish is good, eat a lot of fish in India."

They made a pit stop at the grocery store before going home. Kaccha and her mom cooked dinner while Henry and her dad sat in the living room talking.

" You from South Africa, why leave country? "

" My dad wanted to come to America so that we could have a better life here than back home."

While having dinner Kaccha and Henry explained in great detail why Kaccha found herself in the gully, her stay at the hospital and Henry's kindness for helping and letting her stay at his place.

" We happy you walk by that night, you are a good person, but a lot of bad people in America, happy we leave tomorrow. I give you gift later when finish dinner. "

After dinner Kaccha's father gave Henry a ruby diamond ring.

" Here Henry gift for you for thank you of taking care of daughter, I appreciate, here take, and put in finger. Ring fit in finger, yes? "

" Thank you very generous of you both. "

Kaccha's mom bowed her head in approval, Henry looked at her mom and wondered why she as yet to say a word. Kaccha's dad noticed that Henry was looking at his wife.

" She no talk, nothing to say, where we sleep tonight? "

Her dad was the head of the family, he talked with authority in his voice, Henry was trying to find a way to talk to him about Kaccha not going back to India. It will be a hard nut to crack

" Kaccha ready to leave tomorrow, suitcase packed, yes? "

" No."

" What you mean no, get things ready to take plane home? "

" I do not know how to tell you this, Henry and I have fallen in love, and I want to stay with him."

" No, no, no you come home, marriage already arranged "

Kaccha walked over to Henry and put her hand in his hand.

" Please sir I love your daughter very much. "

" Kaccha, you know about India custom, you come back and marry Arjun, he is waiting for you to return home, marry you, no more talk, you take plane with us tomorrow, I now go to bed very tired, come Suhani, come Kaccha, you sleep on floor next to bed. "

Her dad looked at Henry.

" Good night and no more talk. No people fall in love in short time, impossible. You are kind to let us sleep here but Kaccha going home tomorrow. "

Henry made himself comfortable on the couch, he could not sleep, tossing and turning, he could not bear the thought of Kaccha leaving and probably never see her again. Henry decided in the morning he will keep his ground to prevent Kaccha from boarding the plane tomorrow, after a few hours, he was finally able to fall asleep.

" Henry wake up it is morning time to go to airport."

Henry glanced at Kaccha, her eyes where full of tears. She gave Henry a big hug and a kiss on the cheek. Henry was now crying, as she made her way to the door Henry said.

" Please do not go, there must be a way or something that can be done for you to stay with me. Please do not leave me alone, I love you please."

" Only way Kaccha come home and marry Arjun it is the way of our country, thank you again, maybe we meet again in the future, I do not believe so, but never know, Kaccha will marry Arjun, you find nice American woman and everybody happy. "

Kaccha walked out the door followed by her mom, her dad not far behind them. Henry did not move an inch.

" You do not bring us to airport. "

" No, I cannot let Kaccha go back home. "

" I said last night no more talk Kaccha coming with us, Kaccha call taxi."

When Kaccha and her parents were waiting for the taxi, Henry tried to convince her parents for her to stay. He was not going to the airport too painful to see Kaccha get on the plane.

" You make me mad Henry, wanting to change India way of doing things it is not right, he comes taxi. "

Kaccha gave Henry one last kiss.

" I am so sorry Henry, I love you, I will miss you. "

" So much for holding my ground."

The taxi drove away, Henry made his way back to the house, crying like there was no tomorrow, for him there was no tomorrow without Kaccha. As the days went by Henry was back to his daily routine, go to work, go home, Kaccha was still in his heart.

Henry worked for one month after Kaccha's departure and took a leave of absence. He was getting more and more reclusive, one day there was a knock on the door, Henry rushed to the door hoping it would be Kaccha coming home. When he opened the door to his surprise, Lucas was standing in the doorway. They hugged, Lucas entered the house and saw the mess, dirty dishes, dirty laundry on the floor.

" What are you doing man? Look at this mess, I know you are hurting but there is no excuse to have a filthy place to live and open the windows to get rid of the stench in here. You need to clean this place asap. Good

Lord Henry get a hold of yourself. When was the last time you took a shower, are you still teaching, or you also gave up on your career? "

" I took a leave of absence for a couple of months. "

" Henry, I know it's hard to keep going, but it is during our darkest moments that we must focus to see the light. "

" Easy for you to say, the love of your life is not thousands of miles away, focus on the light you said, the light is too far away for me to reach. I do not have the stamina to keep going, my tank is empty. For the first time in my life, I find someone to love, and she actually loves me for who I am. The pain is unbearable without her. "

" Listen Henry you threw in the towel way to quick, you let him walk all over you without putting up a fight. Roll up your sleeves and prepare to do battle. Go after her, bring her back, you know that Kaccha did not want to go back to India, she wanted to stay, well instead of feeling sorry for yourself. Do something, if you fail, well you can always give yourself a path on the back for trying. So, what do you think? "

" I hear you, but I do not know where to start."

" Come on Henry it's simple do not contact her until you're in India you still have her home phone number, right? "

" Yes, I do."

" Well, what are you waiting for? "

" First of all, I am on leave from work, if I take too long before going back to work, I might lose my job, besides I am broke."

" Already finding excuses, you are not the man I thought you were. Come on man, man up and take charge. For Christ's sake Henry you are going to end up in an insane asylum, if you know what I mean. I came here thinking that it might do you some good with a surprise visit offering you my help, what I see for no reason a broken man, take a step forward and show them what you are made of, I guess inside you are still the little boy the bullies used to pick on in grade school. What a shame. You said your broke, do you have a credit card or a line of credit you can use? "

" Alright that's enough I get the message but like I said I am broke. I do not have a credit card or line of credit. I did not see any purpose to have a credit card or a line of credit. I have to admit right now a line of credit would be useful."

" Let me worry about that, if you decide to go which I hope you do I have a credit card that you can use for your expenses. We will discuss a way for you to pay me back when you come back. Listen Henry, I love you are my brother and it's killing me to see you like that, if you do not stand up for yourself people will always walk all over you for the rest of your days."

" Your right it is time for me to stop whining and do something."

" Go see your doctor and tell him you need more time before going back to work, the school board cannot fire you because you are sick, with the proper paperwork your insurance will keep paying you until you go back to work. Do not tell anybody what your plans are. Go and bring her back. One question have you tried contacting her? "

" Yes, I did, I tried social media, I did not call or write her a letter, in fear that her parents might see the letter or answer the phone if I try calling. "

" You know what Henry, I have a feeling, a hunch that her father may have changed the phone number to make sure you would not be able to reach her, I will call with my cellphone, if they have caller id, he will see my number instead of yours and he might answer, give me the number."

Henry gave Lucas the phone number, when Lucas called, there was a message. The number that you are calling is no longer in service.

" My hunch was right, he switched numbers, listen I have a buddy in my unit we call the hacker I will give him a call, give him the phone number and see if he can find her parents new number, I will be surprised if he is not able to find the number. "

Lucas called his friend, told him about the situation and why he wanted him to try to find the new number.

" Ok I can certainly try what is the number? "

Lucas gave him the number.

" Wow ok that's quite the number."

" India phone number."

" I will try when I get home tonight. "

" Thanks, talk to you later."

" My friend will try tonight to find the new number."

" Thank you, when do you have to go back to the base. "

" In a week, I took some time off because my unit might be deployed to Afghanistan for a one-year tour. I will know when I get back."

" A year in a war zone."

" I will be fine do not worry about me you focus on getting your girl back, let's go grab something to eat."

Later that evening Lucas gets a call.

" That must be my friend, what have you got for me? Yes ok, a text message great, I knew you would be able to find the number, I want to be like you when I grow up, thanks a million, no news yet about our deployment, no see you in a week buddy."

" So, a good call or a bad call"

" Good he was able to find the new number, man that guy is good, he is a computer wiz, in a few minutes he will send me a text message with all the information."

When Lucas received the text message, they were both amazed at the amount of information he was able to find, the new number, her parents address, the description of the house a map of the neighborhood.

" I told you he was good, I love that guy, I would like to know why a computer wiz like him is doing in the army? I do not want to rush you Henry, but call your doctor for an appointment tell him you need to see him asap"

The next morning, Henry called for an appointment to see his doctor,

" Hi, I would like to make an appointment to see the doctor, it is really urgent that I see him. Tomorrow afternoon two o'clock great thank you very much. "

" Two o'clock tomorrow afternoon, perfect, now get on the phone and book a flight to India, I want to make sure that everything is in order for you to go get your girl, do not drop the ball Henry and do not come back without her kapish, now call the airline."

" I wait until I see my doctor tomorrow. "

" Why wait? I am sure that he will give you some extra time off. Here is the phone now call the airline. "

Henry booked a flight for eleven am Wednesday morning.

" Good Henry the day after tomorrow, now get your shit together and start packing, I will call mom and dad to give them the news and to expect me home Wednesday night. "

Lucas called his parents

" They are not home; Hi mom and I am with Henry at his place please call me back on my cellphone. Love you guys. I left a message. "

" Yes, I heard you, thanks."

Lucas was proud of himself to be able to convince Henry to go.

" Have you told them yet that you might be going to Afghanistan? I don't like the fact that you will be in a war zone for a year, are you concerned on how they will take the news? their only son going to war."

" I know, when I enlisted in the army, they were aware that I might be going to war. I forgot to ask you do have a passport up to date? I hope the answer is yes or else we are screwed. "

" Yes, I do have an updated passport. "

" Thank god."

Henry packed his suitcase; they both went to bed. The next morning Lucas said.

" You should get a more comfortable couch, I did not know how to get comfortable, most of the night my body was shaped like a pretzel "

" Tonight, I will sleep on the couch, and you can sleep in my bed. Mr. pretzel."

" Very funny what time is it? "

" Nine am why? "

" let's go somewhere for breakfast. "

While they were having breakfast Lucas phone rang.

" Hi mom nice of you to call me back. I am having breakfast with Henry he is going to see his doctor at two o' clock. No, no, he is not sick, I should say love sick, he is going to talk to the doctor if he can extend his sick leave because I finally convinced him to go get Kaccha, his flight is tomorrow morning eleven am. Yes, I will stay with him until the plane is off the ground and on its way to India, my credit card. Ok love you see you tomorrow night, she wants to talk to you."

" Hi mom, I am looking forward to getting there and nervous at the same time, yes, a twenty-five-hour flight, it will be Thursday night India time when we land. Flight number Indi 60224. I will be careful, yes if I get into trouble I will call you, if not I will talk to you when I get back, yes with Kaccha for sure. Say hi to dad for me and love you both very much, bye bye mom."

" You don't need a phone to call me from India, go to a cyber coffee shop."

" Yes, I know, let's go see the doctor."

Once at the doctor's office, Lucas was getting pretty friendly with the office secretary.

" Ok sir the doctor will see you now. "

" Thank you. "

Fifteen minutes later Henry was done, the secretary gave Lucas her phone number, he winked at Henry, Henry only shook his head.

" Did you see how beautiful she is and also single, broke up with her boyfriend about eight months ago, this will be her first date since her breakup. "

" Now don't go breaking her heart, her first date in eight months, means she was really hurt by the breakup. In case you are interested the doctor gave me a four-month extension. "

" Great you know Henry I do not know if you will understand but I felt some instant karma between the two of us, she might be the one, I have dated a few women in the past year, to be honest it's the first time that I feel this way about a woman, you never know. "

Henry looked at him and said, " You never know my friend you never know."

They drove home, Henry double checked his luggage, made sure everything was in order to avoid delays at customs, they cleaned the apartment. Henry was nervous, it was also his first trip out of the country. Lucas provided Henry with information on how to contact him.

Henry spent a restless night unable to relax and fall asleep. He managed to get two hours sleep at the most. After breakfast, suitcases loaded in the car, Lucas and Henry made their way to the airport. While Henry waited to board the plane, Lucas was a little worried.

" Henry, I have to admit, I am a little nervous to let you go alone, I wish I was going with you. Be careful don't do anything foolish, keep your cool don't act on impulse, use your brain, take the time to think about your next move. "

" I will Lucas, I will take all the necessary precautions so that I can come back home with Kaccha by my side. They just announced my flight number, I need to go board the plane."

They hugged and said their goodbyes

" Thanks a million Lucas I will forever be in your debt, I love you man, be careful if you go to Afghanistan, like you told me do not do anything foolish, do not die on foreign soil in a place where we should not be fighting someone else's war. "

" My intentions are on coming back, take care and do not hesitate to contact me if something happens because if you don't, I will be upset."

Lucas watched Henry walk away to board the plane. He was thinking. I hope he is able to bring her back, I will probably not see him until I get back from Afghanistan. Lucas got in the car and was on his way to Chicago.

CHAPTER 4

After a very long flight Henry finally reached his destination, after claiming his luggage, he took a taxi to his hotel. Once in his room he collapsed on the bed, he was exhausted, he did not get much sleep on the plane, in a matter of minutes Henry was asleep. After a power nap of ten hours, Henry went downstairs to get something to eat.

The attendant told him the dining room was closed for the night, he walked about ten minutes before finding a restaurant that was still open. He indulged in Indian cuisine when done he walked to his hotel with a full belly. Once in his room he was putting together a plan for the next day.

" Tomorrow, I will go to the neighborhood where Kaccha lives, find a place that I can hang out and be able to watch the ins and outs of the place. "

Henry was up at six am, took a taxi to Kaccha's neighborhood. As luck will have it, Henry found a hotel a short distance across the street from Kaccha's house. He booked a room, took another taxi to go get his stuff, checked out of his hotel.

The manager was not pleased, Henry booked the room for a week and after one day he checked out. He grabbed another taxi, checked in his new room, by chance he was able to rent a room on the second floor with one window facing across the street with a perfect view of Kaccha's house.

Henry was really excited, but he would need to be careful when leaving his room and out the hotel door. The first day there was no movement from the house.

The car was parked alongside the house. Disappointed for not having witnessed any movement he went to bed early. He planned on keeping watch from early morning until late at night, not to miss anything. The next morning, he was up bright and early and at his post in the corner of the room which provided him with an excellent view of Kaccha's house.

After an hour of waiting, he saw Kaccha leave the house, Henry's heart was racing a mile a minute, how he wanted to go talk to her, but he needed patience to accomplish his task of bringing Kaccha home. A few minutes later her dad came out of the house, got into his car, backed up from the side of the house and turned left, he said to himself.

" Good Kaccha turned right and walked away, her dad turned left probably to go to work."

He would need to wait until later in the day in order for him to take notes, the hour Kaccha gets home, the time her dad gets home. In the meantime, from his room, he took a good look at Kaccha's house.

India, which is known for small houses, the house was fairly large, nothing fancy on the outside, clay and bricks, small driveway. He came to the conclusion that Kaccha's family was well off compared to the people living in tiny shacks. Not rich but a comfortable life.

The evening could not come fast enough for Henry. He noted Kaccha left the house at seven am. He spotted her walking to her house; he checked his watch five thirty pm. From what Henry could observe by the look on her face Kaccha was sad. Again, he had to hold back his impulsive mind to go and grab her.

He reminded himself patience is a virtue. A couple of minutes pass six o'clock her dad pulled in the driveway. Henry took note of his time of arrival home. All evening Henry was walking back and forth in his room trying to come up with a plan on what to do the next morning, he went to bed with no clue what to do next.

In the morning he decided to keep an eye on the house for one more day, he wanted to make sure he covered all the bases before his next move. Same time seven am Kaccha left the house, took the same direction as the day before. Same thing for her father, came out of the house a few minutes behind Kaccha, jumped in his car, took the same direction from the previous day.

Henri took a chance and ventured out of the hotel to get some fresh air and buy some groceries. His room was equipped with a small fridge and stove. When Henry stepped outside Mrs. Krishenath was outside in front of her house.

She glanced in his direction while waiting for a taxi. Henry kept walking. the taxi drove by and in the corner of his eyes he was able to see Mrs. Krishenath staring at him. Henry walked into a nearby store purchased some groceries, hurried back to his hotel.

Henry was a little peeved at himself for not being more careful before stepping outside. He was upset, what if Suhani was certain, it was him, she saw? Would she tell her husband? Would she keep quiet? Would she let Kaccha know? Was he doomed to fail? Go back home empty handed or end up in jail and not able to go back home?

Mrs. Krishenath returned home before both Kaccha and her dad. Henry was bracing for the worst. Kaccha entered the house at five thirty-five pm and her dad pulled up in the driveway five fifty pm.

Henry now knew it was their daily routine. One hour passed no movement from the house, another two hours went by still nothing.

Henry assumed that Mrs. Krishenath was not sure if it was him that she saw or she just kept quiet.

Henry decided the following morning he will follow Kaccha from a distance to observe where she goes every day. He followed her until she went into a building. He crossed the street from where he was standing, he was able to see Kaccha put on a white laboratory coat.

He retreated across the street, wrote down the address, the name of the building and made his way back to his hotel. Thinking that must be the job that was waiting for her. Again, later in the afternoon like clockwork Kaccha was walking home. He looked at his watch five thirty-two pm, her dad came home five minutes after six o'clock

Now that he knew their schedules, the next morning he would try to talk to Kaccha. He went to bed filled with anticipation, knowing the next morning he would be talking to Kaccha.

The next morning, he was ready to put his plan in action, again he would follow Kaccha from a distance and approach her before she reached the building where she worked. He was not worried about her dad because every morning he takes a different direction.

He was about to make his move when he spotted her dad's car coming down the road. He could not find a place to hide so he turned his back to the street in hope, her dad would not see him. Her dad stopped the car handed a bag to Kaccha, but before driving away he took another glance at the direction of where Henry was on the sidewalk.

He was not able to confirm if it was Henry that he saw. Because Henry hightailed back to his hotel. Kaccha was home when her dad arrived from work. He did not say anything about the possibility, he might have seen Henry across the street where Kaccha works.

He waited until Kaccha was in bed to talk to his wife that Henry might be nearby, following Kaccha to work. They were both speaking in Arabic translated in English.

" Suhani I am pretty sure, Henry was on the other side of the street where Kaccha works, but I am not one hundred percent sure."

" I think I might have seen him yesterday while I was waiting for the taxi, he was walking on the sidewalk across the street, but I am not sure it was him, that is why I did not say anything last night."

" Do not say a thing to Kaccha, she should not know about this, we both saw a man that maybe looks like Henry, yesterday and today. If it is him, he is here for one reason to take Kaccha back to America with him. I will get somebody to discreetly follow Kaccha tomorrow, someone with a camera give me the phone."

Kaccha's dad hired a private investigator to follow Kaccha's every move. So, on the first day following Kaccha the investigator had nothing to report.

" Keep watching if it is him, he is probably going stay quiet for a few days to make us think it was not him. You remember the description I gave you. If it is him, I want to catch him before Kaccha find's out Henry might be in the neighborhood looking for her. She still loves him; she would not hesitate to leave with him. We need to make sure it does not happen."

Back in his room Henry was talking to himself.

" Wow another close call, or was it? What if her father was able to recognize me? For my sake and Kaccha's sake I hope not. Can I be that lucky again? Twice in two days."

The following day Henry decided to stay put for the day, not to draw any suspicion if it was really him, they both saw.

" I am sure they will certainly talk about the fact, Suhani taking a glance at me yesterday and Kumar today."

In the morning Henry positioned himself in the corner of the room so he could see Kaccha walking by. Every morning his heart was really pounding enough to jump out of his chest.

Right on schedule Kaccha came out of the house on her way to work. Henry tried to see if there was any emotion in her face, because of the sun beaming over the building he was only able to get a small glimpse of her face. From what he was able to see, it was the same face that he sees every morning.

He had a notion that there was no discussion about him, until he realized there was a man watching her from a distance, Henry changed position to get a better look, Henry could clearly see a camera in his hands.

" They are not certain it is me they saw, they hired someone to follow Kaccha to and from work. Henry was thinking I better come up with another game plan or risk being detected."

In the meantime, the private investigator was snooping around the neighborhood, without a photo of Henry it will be difficult to make a positive id, the private investigator inquired with the locals if for the last few days, they had noticed a white short man in the neighborhood probably an American.

A lady answered exactly what he wanted to hear. Yes, she has seen a short white man a few times. She was certain to have seen him enter the hotel down the street, armed with new information, he entered the hotel lobby, asked the hotel employee at the front desk if there was a guest at the hotel by the name of Henry Engelbrecht. The clerk turned a few pages in the hotel log book and said in Arabic.

" We do have a guest by that name he checked in five days ago. His room number is 214 on the second floor."

The investigator thanked him for the information he then rushed across the street to Kaccha's house. He knocked at the door. When Kumar answered the door. The investigator was beaming with a big smile.

" I have found him, it is Mr. Engelbrecht, you and your wife have seen in the last few days. A local identified him and told me she had seen him enter the hotel across the street, the clerk at the front desk of the hotel confirmed there is a guest at the hotel by the name of Mr. Engelbrecht."

Kumar told his wife they were both right, it was Henry, he was also seen by a neighbor entering the hotel across the street. He and the investigator will go to the hotel to confront Henry. Kumar advised his wife to not say a word to Kaccha. You can just imagine the surprise when Henry answered the door. Kumar started the conversation.

" Henry what you do here? You no business to be here. You come to take back Kaccha with you, I will have police stop you. Kaccha not know you here will not tell. Now pack go home. You lucky I don't tell police, put you in jail. You have ticket to go back? "

" No not at the moment."

" We wait here, you take phone, buy ticket. I know you love daughter, but she belongs here. She get married in three weeks with good local boy."

Kaccha asked her mom.

" What is going on? Papa was standing in the doorway with a strange man and they went across the street together."

" I do not know."

" Yes, you do, did daddy tell you not to say a word? Does it concern me? "

" I cannot tell you your father will be mad at me."

" I will go see for myself."

Kaccha stormed out the door and crossed the street. Her dad and the investigator were coming out of the hotel.

" Kaccha what are you doing here? Your mother was not supposed to tell you."

" Tell me what daddy? She did not tell me anything, I saw you and him crossing the street. It's Henry he came to India to see me, he is so sweet. I want to see him."

" You will do no such thing, he was here to bring you back to America with him, I made sure, it will not happen, he is taking a plane back home tomorrow."

" Please dad I just want to say hello."

" No come home with me now."

" No, I want to see him."

 She ran to the lobby, started yelling Henry's name, she ran up the stairs, she was now on the second floor. Her dad caught up to her. Henry opened his door to see what the commotion was and spotted Kaccha in the hallway, he ran as fast as he could, grabbed Kaccha in his arms, they kissed.

" I can't believe, you are here. You travelled all the way over here for me wow you really do love me."

" More than you can imagine, I would swim across the ocean knowing, you are on the other side waiting for me."

" I do love you Henry, I miss you terribly, I think about you every day, I am going back with you."

" No, you do not go back with him, I make sure he takes plane tomorrow to go home, my friend stays with him bring him to airport. Now come home. You can cry will not change things he goes home tomorrow."

" Daddy please."

" No, you marry in three weeks, no change plan. Henry, I see you again here you go to jail understand. Now come we go home."

He grabbed Kaccha by the arm and dragged her home. Henry was devastated, he will be going home alone.

" I failed in my quest to bring her home."

The investigator kept an eye on Henry all night. The next morning, he drove Henry to the airport. The only words he said all night and all morning.

" Come on it's time to go to the airport."

Henry had a notion to hit him on the head, make a mad dash, get Kaccha drive like crazy to the airport, but he knew it was not possible. He grabbed his suitcase. Took one final look at the house, with a few tears in his eyes, he was on his way to the airport. I wonder what Lucas will have to say when he finds out I came back home alone.

When his plane landed in San Diego, he was sad and defeated for not bringing her back with him. He was wondering if he would ever see her again. From now on he was sure her family was going to keep a close eye on her, in case I show up again in India.

If Henry only knew Kaccha was planning her own escape to the U. S. after witnessing Henry's efforts to get to her, she was now convinced, they belonged together, she will never be happy if she does not share her life with the man she loves. Deep down she knows it is the right thing to do, leave India for good and enjoy a wonderful life with Henry.

When Henry finished unpacking, he called Lucas.

" Hey buddy back in the States, mission accomplished I hope."

" I am afraid not, one morning her dad spotted me across the street where Kaccha works, he hired a private investigator to keep tabs on me. His investigator escorted me to the airport he made sure I was on a plane home."

" That's too bad, I was really rooting for you. Did you at least have a chance to talk to Kaccha?”

" No well only for a brief moment she was pleading with her dad to let her come back with me. Her dad told me if I ever show my face again in India, he will have me thrown in jail."

" Well, if there's a will there's a way if you two are meant to be together. Do not despair, hope is everything, if you lose hope, you have nothing to live for."

" And you Lucas what about Afghanistan?"

" I leave for fort Bragg tomorrow and Afghanistan in ten days. Do you remember the secretary who works for your doctor, we talked over the phone a few times and that was it? I did not call her back."

" Why? “

" To be honest I don't know why, she was pretty, sweet, maybe because I am leaving for a year, I guess only time would tell, if I did the right thing to not call her again. Now promise me, you are going to get your life back on track, I do not want to be over there dodging bullets worrying about you. I want you to be at the airport to pick me up when I come back."

" No worries I will be there, because you will come back safe and sound. "

" I got to go, I am glad that I was able to talk to you before I leave, do not forget you can always call me via video chat while I am there. I love you man, see you in a year."

" You bet, I love you too brother, how is mom dealing with all of this? “

" She is putting on a brave face for now, probably a different story when I leave tomorrow, take care talk to you soon."

Henry was really depressed, he failed to bring back the love of his life back with him, his best friend, his brother was going in a war zone for a year.

He decided to go visit his parents for a few days. Henry needed a change of scenery. Two days later Henry was on a plane bound for Chicago. His adoptive parents were waiting for him at the airport. With hugs and kisses done, they jumped in the car to go home.

" I am truly sorry Henry that you were not able to bring back Kaccha, so sorry for you my dear. "

" I know thanks mom, at least I tried, I promised myself that I would not leave India without her, I sadly failed, her dad was one step in front of me, I was not able to catch up to him in time."

" So, you mean to tell me this is it, no more attempts, you know Henry some billionaires declared bankruptcy two, three times before succeeding, you would have been a terrible boxer one punch and the fight would have been over."

" What do you want from me dad, I did not come here to be lectured, I wanted to spend time with you guys. Is it a crime failing? Kaccha's dad threatened to put me behind bars for trying to rescue Kaccha, now back home am I going to be condemned for failing? Enough about me what about Lucas going to war? "

His mom replied.

" We rather not think or talk about it. I am going to be like a bouncing ball, until he comes back. "

His dad had this to say.

" We are confident he will come back and your right Henry we are sorry about being on your case, we are also worried about you, we know how deep your love is for Kaccha. We do not like to see you unhappy. So, let's start from scratch, did you have a nice flight? "

After sticking around for a couple of days, Henry decided it was time to go back home to try to put his life back together and take it one day at a time. His mom wanted him to stay a little longer.

" You sure you do not want to stay a little longer? You know you can stay as long as you want."

" I know I have been here for only three days, but I feel I need to go home rebuild my life brick by brick without Kaccha. My flight is scheduled for nine am tomorrow morning. "

" It is a good thing that you are going to pick up the pieces and start fresh, remember only pickup one piece at a time, take the time needed or else you will be overwhelmed and fall flat on your face again. Try to avoid that, because with the size of your nose you might damage a floor or concrete."

" Very funny dad it is so funny I forgot to laugh. I wouldn't talk if I were you, what about the giant ski hill in the middle of your face."

 They were all laughing when his dad said.

" Look at Lisa's honking schnoz, she needs two tissues when she blows her nose, she makes the sound of a blow horn."

Lisa stopped laughing.

" That's not funny, I did not say a word about the door knob in the middle of your face. "

Henry laughing replied.

" You have to admit dad, door knob that's a good one."

" Wha, wha,wha whatever ."

His mom replied.

" Like the movie says, you can't handle the truth. "

" Ok, ok now cut the comedy act and what's for dinner? "

" A new recipe, the aroma is guaranteed that your big nostrils will enjoy, and don't you dare poke your nose in my kitchen while I am cooking you too Henry keep your nose out of my kitchen."

They enjoyed a wonderful dinner still firing friendly insults to one and another, they spent the evening talking about the good old days and how life is not always fair, about Lucas being a soldier serving his country on foreign soil. Mr. Moore looked at his watch

" Time to hit the sack, looking at Henry " you have a flight to catch in the morning, good night, everyone."

" I will pray for you Henry those things turn for the better for you."

" I appreciate that mom but save your prayers for Lucas, he is going to need them a lot more than me."

Henry gave his mom a hug

" Good night mom see you in the morning."

The next morning suitcases packed Henry was ready to go back home. Mr. Moore drove him to the airport, when Henry was about to board the plane Mr. Moore said.

" Don't be a stranger now, do not hesitate to call if you need anything. Love you, hopefully we will see you soon. "

" Thanks dad look after yourself and mom, we will talk soon."

Henry boarded the plane to go home. Wondering what to do or where to start when he gets home. So many questions, so few answers. He drifted off to sleep. He woke up a few minutes before the plane was to land. When home he said to himself

" Now what? "

He sat on the couch and fell asleep. He slept for a couple of hours, once awake he grabbed something to eat, then off to bed. The next morning, he was wondering what to do.

" Today is the day that I am supposed to start pulling myself together easier said than done."

He started by cleaning his place, eating better, going out more often for some fresh air, but he could not take his mind of Kaccha. Little did he know Kaccha was planning to leave India to join him in the U.S.

Using a fake passport. She secretly bought a ticket for a flight to the States, two days before she was to marry a man she never met. On the morning of her flight, she did the same thing as usual walk to work. Every day she would bring personal items to work without her mom or dad noticing.

She was ready. She could barely hide her excitement; she was leaving her homeland to be with Henry. She was also sad, feeling guilty to begin her journey in the States without telling her mom and dad, not having the chance to say goodbye. But it was the only way to do it. That morning her dad talked about the upcoming wedding in a couple days.

" Kaccha today is your final day of work before getting married the day after tomorrow."

" Yes dad."

" Good tomorrow we will make the final arrangements for the wedding. Your future husband is anxious to be able to marry you. He is a good young man; he comes from a very good family."

She could not look her parents in the face, she was feeling horrible for deceiving them, because this was probably the last time, she will see both her mom and dad. Before leaving for work, like every morning she kissed her mother, and her father grabbed her bag and out the house for the final time.

She will miss the house she grew up in but her love for Henry was too powerful for not to be by his side. After a couple of weeks when Henry boarded the plane to go back home, her dad's suspicions that Henry might try a second time to come back to get Kaccha faded away.

There were no signs of Henry coming back to take Kaccha away. He told the private investigator he was no longer needed. That was a big relief for Kaccha. She walked around the corner covered her face, took a taxi. Stopped to get her personal stuff in a locker she rented not too far from work, and she was on her way to the airport.

When the plane left the tarmac she took a long deep breath, so far everything is going according to plan she kept her face covered. When her plane landed, she took a taxi. She kept her face covered until she reached her apartment.

Since arriving in the "U.S" going outside she would always cover her face because she knew her dad would be relentless trying to find her. She did not want anybody to see her face, so she dressed like a muslin.

She used a different name; a fake passport also used her fake name when she rented her place a few weeks before leaving. She was lucky to find a furnished apartment at a modest price.

She was now safe and sound in Tampa Florida. Everything was all set she saved enough money for rent and food for three months. She will only call Henry when she is certain that the coast is clear. She was well aware, her dad will go berserk, using every trick in the book to locate her.

" Finally, she was in her place in the States, she was able to uncover her face and breathe a sigh of relief. She locked the door, stood in the middle of the room for a few minutes. She could not believe she was able to pull it off without a glitch. Covered her face again and took a walk to the corner store to get some groceries.

" She was happy that she took the time to exchange her Indian rupees for United States money. She could just imagine the confusion for the poor clerk at the corner store when she wanted to pay for her things.

After having a little something to eat she took a shower and in bed for the night. She was exhausted after spending twenty-four hours in a plane. It did not take her long to be in snooze land. In the meantime, her dad was trying to find out what was going on. The morning Kaccha boarded the plane bound for the U.S. her employer called the house to advise her mother that Kaccha did not show up for work.

Her mother immediately called her husband to let him know Kaccha was not at work. He drove home, called her place of work. Her boss told him she did not see Kaccha or heard from her all morning, maybe she was confused about her last day of work before the wedding. Talking in Arabic.

" No, she did not seem to be confused at all this morning, she kissed her mother, told us see you tonight. "

They looked in her room and did not find anything out of the ordinary. She was clever, she replaced the personal things she took with her so it would seem that nothing was missing in her room. She did not bring any of her clothes.

She purchased new clothes that she kept hidden in her locker. She was proud of herself, no one was aware of her plans not even her best friend at work. Her motto was loose lips, sinks ships.

Her parents called the police, they talked to potential witnesses without success, no one had seen her. They checked at the airport, bus terminals, passenger ship companies, cruise lines, private airports, small airports.

Police was now thinking maybe a kidnapping, a murder, or she might be hiding somewhere and did not want to be found, she might have eloped with another man? Kaccha's dad was certain that Henry was involved. The same day Kaccha was reported missing he called Henry. He was surprised when Henry answered the phone.

" Henry where Kaccha go, she meets you somewhere yes. "

" I am sorry is this some kind of joke.? I do not know who you are if this is your idea of a joke it is not funny."

" No Henry Kaccha father, Kaccha missing no work today, what you know of this? If not want get hurt, you tell where Kaccha going. "

" Mr. Krishenath you mean to tell me, Kaccha is missing?"

" Yes, you confess what Kaccha doing."

" Please sir start from the beginning, you mean to tell me that Kaccha did not go to work? "

" Yes, you plan with her."

" No, I did not, I will go to India to help you find her."

" You no come here I go to America look for Kaccha. I go tomorrow Kaccha in States by then."

" You are more than welcome sir, but I can assure you, I have not been in contact with Kaccha since leaving India. "

" I no believe you."

" No offense sir but should you be searching for her instead of arguing with me. "

" Kaccha no more home she goes to America for you. "

Mr. krishenath ended the call. Henry was wondering what the hell was going on. Kaccha gone missing and no word from her. Henry was concerned for her safety. If I go to India, her dad will have me arrested.

A few days went by still no word from Kaccha. The doorbell rang. Henry ran to answer the door thinking it might be Kaccha. When he opened the door Kumar pushed Henry to get in the house.

" Where daughter hiding? If you no tell me I call police, I say you kidnap Kaccha. This makes her mother cry a lot. "

" Sir like I said the other day on the phone I have no clue where she is. I do not have any contact with her."

Kaccha's dad searched the house and could not find her or any of her belongings.

" Maybe hide someplace else, I stay here in States until she hides no more. I go rent room. Come here in day see if Kaccha come here. Also watch during night."

" You are welcomed to stay, but you will be wasting your time."

" I no waste time she come from hiding. "

Henry could not convince Kaccha's dad that he did not know Kaccha's whereabouts, he wished he did know because not knowing was driving him crazy. After a few days, still no word from Kaccha. Her dad called home, still no news to her whereabouts. After a week of waiting, he decided to go back home.

" I go home tomorrow, you tell truth Kaccha not here. If you get news, you contact me. Ok I go to hotel, on plane tomorrow for home. "

In the morning Mr. Krishenath was on a plane to go back home. Henry was worried sick not knowing where Kaccha might be. He was hoping, she would contact him to let him know she was ok. Henry called his parents to tell them the news. Mr Moore answered the phone.

" Hi dad."

" Henry."

" Yes, dad it's me. I am calling to let you know Kaccha is gone, nobody knows where she is."

" She is gone, you mean disappeared without a trace. Strange why would she do that? "

" I don't know dad to me it does not make any sense, I keep hoping that she will appear at my door."

" What about in India, no word? "

" No."

" I wonder if they did find her and not wanting to admit it? "

" I do not know dad, but I am worried sick."

" Do you want to talk to your mother?"

" No, I really do not have much to say. Can you say hi for me please?"

" Of course, well good luck in finding her keep me posted please."

" I will dad."

A few weeks went by Henry was still in the dark, not knowing was eating him alive where could she be? After three weeks Kaccha could not wait any longer to contact Henry. She was eager to be in his arms, what really preoccupied her mind was how Henry was coping by not knowing.

It was cruel not to let him know she was ok. She knew for certain that her dad contacted Henry. She decided to take a chance and called Henry via video calling from a cyber cafe. When Henry realized it was Kaccha, he was like a kid in a candy store, he could not hold back his emotions.

" Kaccha, what's happening where are you? "

" Listen Henry sorry for doing this, to make you worry but it was the only thing I could think of to put my plan in motion, I cannot talk very long in case someone can see my face, I am in the United States safe and sound, I just wanted to let you know, I cannot wait to see you but it will have to wait. I love you, soon we will be together for ever. Gotta go. "

Henry was estatic to know that she was alive and well, his biggest surprise she was in the States. He needed to control his emotions until he talked to her again. In India her dad and the police exhausted every avenue possible to find Kaccha, her parents were losing hope of finding her alive.

Her father decided to pay another surprise visit to Henry, thinking that Kaccha might be with him. He took the earliest flight he could get. Again, when Henry opened his door, he was shocked that it was Kumar standing at the door.

" Henry, I come back, see if you hiding Kaccha, can I come in house please? "

" Yes, sir no problem. Nothing changed since the last time you were here sir feel free to look around."

" I get police to check phone calls. "

" Good luck on that one sir. I myself sir I am trying to cope with the possibility something real bad as happened to Kaccha, please sir believe me when I tell you this, you may not like me for what I tried to do but I have nothing to do with her gone missing, I am going crazy not knowing, you know I love your daughter, I would never do anything to arm her, like I said before for some reason if I do hear from her sir, I will let you know, I can see the anguish on your face it must be horrible for you and your wife not knowing as well, we can only hope she will be found alive or show up someday. "

" Me stay two days."

" Stay here with me for two days, alright if that's what it takes to prove to you, I have no idea where Kaccha might be. "

Henry was afraid Kaccha might try to contact him again, that would be devastating for both, plans and their future down the drain. The next day the phone rings, Kumar runs to answer the phone. It was Mrs. Moore calling.

" That you Kaccha? "

" Excuse me who am I talking to? "

Henry grabs the phone.

" Henry is that you? Who answered the phone? "

" Mr. Krishenath, he has come back for a few days. He is still convinced that I am involved with the disappearance of his daughter."

" She is still missing; goodness I hope they find her soon safe and sound. Anyway, my reason for calling. Lucas called, he told me that he was promoted to corporal and changing units, he is now part of a combat patrol unit. That means he is going to be in arms way on a daily basis. That's frightening news don't you think?"

" Yes, it is, but knowing Lucas, he will be very careful, now that he is a officer, he will not try anything stupid to get his men in a bad situation take a risk to get some of his men killed or wounded. How long has he been in country now?

" He has been gone now for almost two months; your dad said the same thing you just told me. He will be careful. "

" How do Julie and Nicole feel about their baby brother fighting a war?"

" I talked to them about a week ago, they will pray for God to watch over him, they still feel guilty for not being here when he departed for Afghanistan. Anyway, Henry, I will let you go, keep praying and hoping that you will see Kaccha again someday, and good luck with her dad."

The next day Henry drove his future father-in-law to the airport. Chances are that he will never see him again. He was ok with that.

" Thank you to bring me to airport, you tell truth not know where is Kaccha, I have proof you no lie to me. If I get news, I call to give you news."

" Thank you I would love that. Goodbye now and have a safe flight home Mr. Krishenath."

Henry could finally breathe a sigh of relief, Kaccha's dad was gone. If Kaccha would have called when her dad was at his place, they were both doomed. He was also happy, Kumar does not suspect him anymore. Now all he had to do is go home and wait for the call from Kaccha and hopefully reunite soon. His wait was almost over.

CHAPTER 5

Five days after her dad supposedly took a flight home Kaccha contacted Henry, again from a cyber cafe.

" Hello Henry, how are you? I miss you."

" Hello my love, I have great news, your dad was here a week ago double checking if I knew your whereabouts."

" Excuse me Henry what does that word mean."

" Sorry honey, I should be more careful in my choice of words. He was double checking if I knew where you were and if I had any contact with you. When I drove him to the airport, he told me I was off the hook, meaning he believed me, I had nothing to do with you missing. It was not a great feeling to give a man false information when it concerns his daughter. "

" Henry my dad was more preoccupied to make sure that I marry a man I never met, because he is the son of a very wealthy man. He was more concerned about filling his pockets, I was like a bargaining tool for him. So do not feel guilty. Like you Americans say we have the green light to start planning our future. This is the moment I have been dreaming about since I was forced to go back home."

" Ok my love what is the plan that you have in mind. I hope it is a short one so we can be soon in each other's arms. "

" Henry it just occurred to me, my dad might have tricked you to believe he was going back to India, he might still be in San Diego watching your house."

" Do you really think so? I drove him to the airport; your dad was on the plane when it took off for India."

" He led you to believe, he was leaving, telling you that he was now certain, you were not a suspect anymore. To me it does not sound right. I know my dad he has done many under handing things in his life, this one would not be different. "

" Well, what do we do now?"

" Do you have many lady friends at work? "

" A few why? "

" Well, I have an idea, could one of your lady friends do you a favor?"

" Yes, I think so. "

" Ask your friend if she would be willing to participate in a little scheme that would help us determine if my dad is still watching your house. If she says yes. Tell her to wear what you call a hoodie I think that's the name a hoodie and walk fast to your house please call me back to let me know, my number 123-555-1003. "

" Now I get it, if your dad is still watching the house, he will come running thinking it is you. When she comes in, I will tell her to go in the bathroom, I will give her a call. "

" Call her soon please, I am eager for us to finally be a couple. "

" I will call her tonight."

Henry contacted his lady friend, gave her all the details needed to pull off the stunt. She agreed, it would be for the following night around six o'clock. Everything was set to put their plan in motion. Henry called Kaccha to let her know that it was a go.

" Kaccha my love, my lady friend is willing to help. She will be knocking at my door tomorrow evening. "

" I can't wait to find out what will happen. "

" Me too, talk to you soon."

When Henry ended the call, he was thinking what a smart little bird my Kaccha, brilliant plan, I can't wait for tomorrow night. Like clockwork the lady friend rang the doorbell, Henry let her in, she headed straight to the bathroom. Kumar noticed Henry's lady friend walk to the house and Henry let her in. He yelled out loud.

" I right, catch you,"

He ran to the house, burst open the door.

" Where Kaccha, see her come in house, you think smarter than me, you lie to me all the time."

Kumar detected some noise coming from the bathroom. Kumar was banging on the bathroom door, when the door opened, to his surprise it was not Kaccha.

" Kumar what are you still doing here, aren't you supposed to be in India? What is the big idea, bursting into my house like that? You told me that. "

" I know what I say to you. It a trick to fool you think gone back home. "

" Kumar I would like to introduce you to my fellow colleague and friend Natasha. I invited her over for coffee and catch up on the news at work. Do you want to sit down and have a coffee with us?"

Kumar shook his head no,

" No, I go now but why Henry you no work stay in house all day, you waiting for Kaccha?

" Mr. Krishenath you must know now I am telling you the truth; I am insulted, you did not take my word. Do you see now, proof I am honest in what I tell you, oh yes sir, one more thing if you ever put another foot on my property, not even a toe nail I will have you arrested. It's getting ridiculous. You should be in India helping the police to try to locate Kaccha. I have accepted that I will never be able to be with her. Please sir leave my house."

Kumar lowered his head, did not apologize he was about to say something, changed his mind and he was out the door.

" Good riddance, I cannot thank you enough Natasha for what you did for me tonight. "

" No problem it was fun to see the expression on his face, boy quite the character of a man that guy, when are you coming back to work Henry, we all miss you?"

" Soon I hope, coffee before you leave? "

" Yes, thank you."

" If I recall cream but no sugar. "

" Yes sir. "

" I do not know if he will give up after tonight, take your time drinking your coffee the longer you are here the better, in case he is still keeping an eye on the house to see what time you will be leaving, once outside I will give you a hug and a kiss on the cheek. Is that, ok?"

" Hoooooo Henry of course, I did not know there would be fringe benefits. Hoooola henri mon cheri. "

" Ha ha very funny, your husband is six two, two hundred twenty pounds, look a me, I am a little squirt compared to him, he would squash me like a bug."

" It's good to see you laugh again, ten o'clock time for me to leave. We are all eager to see you back at work."

Henry escorted Natasha to the door, on the front porch he kissed her on the cheek with a nice big hug.

" Ho henri mon cheri."

" Good night, Natasha and thanks again I owe you one."

" Well of course mon cheri."

He watched Natasha walk away, closed the door and called Kaccha.

" So, Henry was I right about my dad?"

" Ho yes indeed, as soon as Natasha was in the house, there he was as soon as he set foot in the house, he started yelling Kaccha show yourself I know you are here. The look on his face when Natasha came out of the bathroom was priceless, I wish I had a camera. Natasha was here until ten o'clock when she left the house, outside in plain view of everybody, whoever was watching was able to see the hug and the kiss on her cheek."

" After this episode, I am sure my dad will go back home, he will not waste any more time and money on a dead horse. Ok so Henry we need to talk, can you come to Tampa Bay to see me, my funds are limited at the moment, I might not have the money to pay for the trip to go see you."

" I will be there the day after tomorrow, probably in the afternoon. What are your coordinates?"

" Sorry Henry my what?"

" Geez sorry again for using such big words, I mean your address. Question, are you going to stay in the states with a false name and passport? "

" Henry I am a chemist I brought with me everything that I need to make it legal for me to stay in the state. I cannot wait to see you."

The next morning after a quick breakfast, Henry was on his way to see Kaccha. He programmed his GPS with her address. As far as he was concerned so far it was the happiest day of his life. He was so excited that he did not take the time to call Mrs. Moore to give her the news and his whereabouts for the coming week.

Henry was speeding down the highway, busy thinking that he will be in Kaccha's arms soon, planning their future. He will be in heaven, he will be marrying an angel, to notice how fast he was going, the red and blue lights behind him brought him back to reality. Henry pulls over, the cop walks to his car.

" Good afternoon, sir do you know why I pulled you over?"

" Speeding."

" That's right, I clocked you at one hundred thirty in a zone of ninety miles an hour. You're going to have to remove the concrete in your boots my friend. License and registration please."

Henry reached in the glove compartment, handed over the registration of the car, reached in his wallet, retrieved his driver's license

" There you go officer. "

" Thank you I will be right back."

It only took the officer a few minutes to walk back to Henry's car

" Wow that was fast."

" New technology makes a job a lot easier. I have bad news sir, your driver's license expired, six weeks ago."

" You have got to be kidding me, six weeks ago."

" That's right sir here is the situation, I checked your driving record, clean slate, why were you speeding today?

" I am on the last leg of a thirty-four-hour drive. To be honest sir, I did not realize how fast I was going, you see I am going to join my girlfriend in Tampa. If you only knew the road, I had to take to get to her. I was not concentrating on anything else but to get to her. We could be sitting at a table sipping coffee, all afternoon while I talk about my journey. Sorry officer I am babbling away here. "

" Must be some story."

" You better believe it my friend."

" Ok now I could fine you for speeding, driving with an expired license. You seem to be a nice guy, here what I will do, I will forget the fine for driving with an expired driver's license, I will reduce your speeding ticket to only twenty miles over the speed limit. But as soon as you get to Tampa, please go renew your driver's license. In case you get pulled over again this is a paper for you when you get to Tampa you are to go to the license bureau and get your driving license up to date. It must be some story, speeding forgetting to renew your license especially for a guy like you with such a clean driving record. If you don't mind my asking sir, what do you do for a living? "

" I am a high school teacher. "

" What do you teach?"

" Law, ha ha ha no I teach math. "

" Ok sir I would love to stay and chat, but I have a job to do, and you have to get to Tampa. All the best for you and your girl. "

Henry extended his arm and shook hands with the police officer,

" I have the most respect for police officers putting their lives on the line to protect us. I can see that you are a good man with a big heart. Take care and stay safe, Tampa is forty-five minutes away, good I will be there in twenty."

The police officer said with a smile.

" I am going to have to keep an eye on you. "

" Wow what a nice officer, I was lucky that he is the one that pulled me over?"

Henry took a long deep breath.

" Omigosh me speeding, not renewing my driver's license. When I get to Tampa, first thing I am going to do is check if my head is still screwed on tight on my shoulders. I do not know how many times drivers shouted at me get off the road granny. Yahoo Kaccha here I come. "

When Henry arrived, Kaccha came running, pulled Henry out of the car, embracing him.

" I am never letting go, I love you so much, it was horrible to be in India and you here, I never want to be away from you again. I cannot believe that you are here my love."

Henry was finally able to close the car door, they hugged and kissed.

" Thank god this is what I was praying for Henry to be in your loving arms. "

They slowly walked hand in hand to the house and cuddled on the couch.

" Kaccha my love I won the lottery today you're in my arms. "

" Thank you that is so sweet."

After the cuddling session was over, Henry brought his luggage in the apartment. They celebrated by going out for dinner. After dinner they cuddled again on the couch.

" Henry I am scared to go out at night, because of what happened."

" We will go for a stroll every night until you are again comfortable to go out at night."

" Ok."

Has promised when they were settled in Henry's house. Henry would take Kaccha for a walk every night after dinner until her fear of being outside after dark was gone.

" I was so anxious and impatient to get here, I was pulled over for speeding for the first time in my life, I forgot to renew my license, I was lucky, the cop who pulled me over was a real gentleman, a really nice down to earth man. He could have nailed me for driving with an expired license, he reduced my speeding ticket to only twenty miles over the limit. Tomorrow, I have to go to the license bureau to get my license renewed. This is so nice if we could only freeze this moment."

" Yes, it would be so nice to be able to do that. It is getting late; I want to go to bed. "

" What are the sleeping arrangements?"

" We are not in India, we are in America, it is not illegal to share the same bed with your man before getting married. This is only a one-bedroom apartment, you did not come all the way over here to sleep on a couch. I am going to take a shower and get ready for bed."

When Kaccha entered the bedroom, Henry was sprawled on the bed sleeping. She covered him with a blanket. She slipped into bed alongside Henry. The next morning Henry was embarrassed for quickly falling asleep. They walked to a nice little restaurant down the street to have breakfast.

After breakfast Henry took a drive to the license bureau to renew his driver's license. When he was done at the license bureau, he stopped at a flower shop purchased twelve roses. When he returned home Kaccha was in the bedroom. He slowly walked in the bedroom with the bouquet of roses.

" This is for you, my darling every rose represents one of the twelve months of the year, meaning I will always be by your side no matter what, I will always do whatever it takes so we can be together forever that's a promise I will never break, no matter the cost. "

" Thank you so much, you are so sweet, I will love you forever."

" I know, like every couple we will have our ups and downs, the only thing to remember is what brought us together and what keeps our love for one another strong."

" Henry, I have a visiting visa for only ninety days, I will have to leave when it expires. What are we going to do? I rented this place for only three months. "

" You know how much I love you and I will always love you."

" Yes of course I do, your love for me was proven when you tried to get to me and bring me back from India with you. That my dear Henry I will never forget what you did for me."

Henry goes down on one knee

" Will you marry me, I know we've only known each other for a short period of time, but I know you are my soulmate, I do not want to spend another minute without you. I did not get the chance to buy you an engagement ring yet, but if you say yes, we will go shopping for a nice ring for you

" Yes, yes, and yes, I will marry you, no need to get a ring they are very expensive. We need to be careful on how we spend the money until I can get a work visa."

" We have a period of three months to get married, then you can apply for a green card and eventually apply for U.S citizenship. "

" What do we do now? Like I said I rented this place for three months, do I stay here until we get married, or I go home with you, I did not know we would be able to share the same home so quick. "

" Do you want me to stay here with you or go home to San Diego?"

" I want to go to San Diego with you, because that is where we can start building our lives but what do I do with this place?"

" Have you paid for the full three months?"

" No only two months."

" Did you sign a lease?"

" No, only month to month. "

" Pack your bags honey we are leaving in the morning; we will drop the key to the landlord when we leave. "

That night they cuddled in bed, until they both fell asleep. Henry and Kaccha decided to wait for their wedding night to make love. The next morning, with their stuff in the car, they drove to the office of the landlord, hung the key on the door with a little note that Kaccha will not be coming back.

" Buckle up honey it's a long, long, very long drive, I will drive ten hours today, another ten tomorrow and then all the way home without stopping except for munchies and bathroom breaks."

Kaccha was looking at Henry with excitement and anticipation.

" Kaccha when we get home, we will look into getting you a marriage visa, second step a green card and eventually apply for U. S citizenship. To comply with the United States law, we need to get married within the ninety days. "

" Wow all of that."

" I know but it's not done in one day, there is a time frame to follow, we will eventually get to the finish line. I call it the marathon of happiness one day at a time. "

After a long ten-hour drive, they stopped at a motel for the night, a quick bite to eat and off to bed. The next morning a quick breakfast, like the Willy Nelson song (on the road again).

Another long day of driving, another motel a quick bite to eat and hit the sack. In the morning again a quick breakfast, hit the road hoping to make it all the way to San Diego without having to stop again to catch some zzzzzz's

" Today honey I hope to be able to drive until we get home, we have about a fourteen-hour drive ahead. You know if I get too tired of driving, cruise control will get us home."

" We are not in an airplane where you can activate the autopilot silly you. I will also need to get a driver's license."

" Yes, all in due time."

Henry looked at his watch.

" We still have a long way to go Henry?"

" Only another nine hours of driving. Boy, am I going to be happy when the car is parked in the driveway?"

" Do you think I will be able to find work in San Diego?"

" Absolutely, with your bachelor's degree in chemistry and biology, you will be working in no time."

The final hours of the trip. As if time was standing still, not making any progress, Kaccha was asleep. Henry was gulping down the coffee to stay awake. Finally, after fourteen long hours of driving they finally made it home.

" Kaccha wake up we are home, boy the driveway never looked so good, leave everything in the car, we can take care of that in the morning. I am exhausted."

Henry unlocked the door, Kaccha dashed for the bedroom, Henry to the bathroom, when he entered the bedroom Kaccha said.

" Good night. "

As soon as she closed her eyes, she was asleep. Henry was thinking, man what a relief to finally be home, we can sleep in tomorrow morning. The miles that I do in a year I did in six days. The next morning there was a knock on the door. Henry answered the door he stood there in shock. There he was Kumar standing at the door. Henry could not believe his eyes. Kumar pushed Henry out of his way.

Kaccha was in the kitchen cooking breakfast.

" Kaccha, I know you here, come here. "

" Father what are you doing here? Please leave me alone this is the life I have chosen you need to accept the fact that I am staying here with Henry. "

Kumar looked at Henry.

" You fool you tell lies to me, me smarter, made believe, I trust you, you lie, I lie. Come home now, this not life plan for you. You obey India culture. I not leaving, stay here, when you ready come home, I leave with you, and you think smart. I stay at hotel, pay a man watch house. I now get you. I call police arrest you put in jail."

" Mr. Krishenath, with all due respect sir, you cannot do anything she is here on her own free will. Kaccha show your dad your visiting visa, we did not break any laws."

" I no talk to you anymore, you in India you dead."

" Kumar did I not warn you if you were to come back here, I would have you arrested for trespassing. "

" Father go home, leave me alone, I do not love you anymore, you want me to go back and marry the man chosen for me, so you can get some money, because his parents have a lot of money, I do not want to see you anymore, please leave. "

He stepped outside; Kumar stepped back in the house with two men.

" I know you not come with me; I pay men to bring you with me to India."

" Kumar you cannot do that; this is not India. "

" I tell you no talk to you, now Kaccha go to bedroom get stuff we are leaving. "

Henry called 911, it only took a few minutes for the cops to arrive.

" Henry, you call police, you fool I tell them you steal daughter; you go to jail. "

Two police officers entered the house, one of the officers was pointing to Henry.

" Sir are you the one who called 911? "

" Yes."

" Ok now can you tell me what is going on here."

" Kumar started babbling away."

" Sir I am not talking to you; I am talking to the gentleman so let the man talk. "

" You no understand, he steals daughter."

" Sir this is your last warning, if you do not let him explain to me why we are here, you are going to end up in the back seat of our police car. Now sit down and be quiet. "

" Kaccha was standing in the corner crying, Henry explained everything to the police officer his partner was taking notes. He looked at Kaccha

" Miss, can you show me your visiting visa, your passport, please. "

Kaccha handed over the documents to the police officer. After looking over her documents, with what Henry told him and the documents that Kaccha provided, he was starting to get a clear picture of what was going on, Kaccha told the police officer her story.

" Ok well I can see you were here on a student visa as well; you did not have any problems applying for both visas that I am looking at right now."

" No sir I did not. "

He turned around to face Kumar.

" So, sir what is your excuse to be here? "

When Kumar was finished talking the police officer said

" Let me educate you on American laws sir, you cannot do what you are trying to do. It is against the law.

" It no against law, she is daughter to me, what you are talking about, Henry gave money to you for me to leave? I not leaving."

" Sir I am trying to explain to you what you can do and what you cannot do. Do you realize you accused me of fraud, taking money from someone to illegally do something in their favor? It is a crime, so be careful what you say sir, you might end up in jail."

" How me in jail. He criminal take away daughter? "

" Sir what are these men doing here? "

" I pay them to help get Kaccha on plane go home. "

" Really you paid them to help you kidnap your daughter. "

" Not kidnap bring daughter home."

" Your friends are being arrested for conspiracy to kidnapping. Peter call dispatch, tell them we need assistance here and to send backup."

A few minutes later a police cruiser arrived, the police officers were filled in on the situation to arrest the two men and bring them to the station. Kumar's two partners in crime were taken away in handcuffs.

" Why bring them to jail they do nothing wrong?"

" Never mind those two, you should be more concerned about yourself. Now it is your turn, can I see your paperwork sir and your passport. "

Kumar's face had the look of someone that was really annoyed. He handed over his documents to the officer. When the officer was done looking over Kumar's documents. He said.

" For what I can see here sir, you are breaking the law, not them."

" What you mean I give you papers, I no resist to give papers? "

" I thank you for that, but at the airport you told the agents that you were on a five-day business trip. That means after five days you were supposed to go back home, the second misdemeanor which means your second offense you provided a false statement when you declared you were here on a business trip, the third offense is you are trying to get someone to go with you against her own free will. In the U.S. we call it kidnapping which is a criminal offense. You could be behind bars for a very long time. "

" I know nothing of this. All I want to bring daughter back home, you tell me I go to jail, I no understand. "

Kaccha and Henry waved to the officer, they wanted to talk to him.

" You stay here, do not move I will be right back. "

The officer joined both Kaccha and Henry in the kitchen.

" What's up?"

" We were thinking why not send him back to India with a stern warning that he is never to come back in the states or else he will be thrown in jail. With his name and photo in the database, he will not be able to enter the United States."

" I cannot let him go with just a warning, what you are asking me will need to be decided by a judge. I have to bring him to the precinct; his photo and fingerprints will be taken. He is going to be in jail until he goes in front of a judge, the judge will decide his fate. "

" How long do you think it will take before he is in front of a judge?"

" Usually a few days, that's when the judge decides to grant the accused to go free on bail, keep him in jail or dismiss the case for a lack of evidence. You can testify on his behalf."

He motioned to his partner to put the cuffs on Kumar and take him away.

" Kaccha I no understand I go to jail, what mother say?"

Kaccha was crying and put her head on Henry's shoulder, she could not bear to see her dad being whisked away in handcuffs.

" Kaccha one of the teachers at school her husband is a lawyer, I will give her a call. "

" Thank you, I did not know that things would be such a mess. I was certain that my dad would have given up and gone back to India by now. "

A few days later Kumar was in court, with Kaccha and Henry's testimony and a very convincing lawyer. Kumar was able to go back to India with one exception to never contact Kaccha again and never come back to the states. He was on a flight home the following day. Kaccha and Henry were happy it was over and to be able to concentrate with the steps needed to keep Kaccha in the states.

Kaccha and Henry retained the services of the lawyer to make sure not to have any hiccups and delays to resolve everything that needed to be done in order for Kaccha to remain in the states. Henry contacted his parents to give them the latest news and inquired on how Lucas was doing in Afghanistan.

Henry and Kaccha bought a house to another part of town, to get away from the bad memories of her dad trying to bring her back home. With a work visa Kaccha was able to find employment at a chemical research company. Henry returned to work.

Kaccha was happy with the papers she falsified did the trick.

His first day back at work Henry received a warm welcome from his colleagues. As time went on, all the paperwork done and approved, Kaccha and Henry married, a small wedding attended by coworkers, a few friends and his family.

Mr. Moore walked Kaccha down the aisle. Mrs. Moore walked down the aisle with Henry. Julie and Nicole were both maids of honor, Henry's close friend from work was his best man. Unfortunately, Lucas was not able to attend the wedding.

After the wedding ceremony, they all headed to a nice restaurant where reservations were made in advance and enjoy a nice dinner. When dinner was done. The newlyweds drove to the motel where a reserved honeymoon suite was waiting for them to finally be able to enjoy their first night as a married couple. They were both on cloud nine.

CHAPTER 6

When Henry said the words until death do us part. That's a promise that he will never break, no matter the cost. He loved Kaccha, his love for her was for all eternity. Luca's tour of duty was over he came back home with his new girlfriend. They met in Afghanistan, she was a combat medic. They met in a bar on the base, and they have been a couple ever since. Lucas introduced her to his parents.

" Mom, dad I would like to introduce you to the girl who stole my heart. Sandra my parents. "

" Nice to meet you, how long have you two known each other?"

" Four months, why do you ask dad?"

" Nothing just curious that's all. Last time we spoke you did not mention anything about having a girlfriend."

" How is my baby brother doing? I did not get to many chances to contact him."

" How was it over there, did a lot of your friends get hurt?"

" Well mom it was no walk in the park that is for sure, some days where good and some well I would rather not talk about, four of my buddies were killed in action and over a dozen wounded. I am one of the lucky ones to come back without a scratch."

" And you Sandra you were in the thick of things, dodging bullets to save your fellow marines? "

" Yes, I was sir, I did my best to keep them alive."

" I am sure you did, where are you from Sandra?"

" I am from Detroit Michigan."

" Mom, dad I asked you guys a little while ago how is Henry doing?"

" Well sit-down son, we have one heck of a story to tell you."

The next day Lucas called Henry, when Henry answered the phone, he was excited and happy to hear Lucas voice at the other end of the line.

" Hey little brother, how are you doing, mom and dad told me about your adventures, is everything still quiet?"

They talked for about an hour, Lucas mentioned he was going to visit his little brother in about a week. Sweet music to Henry's hears, he was anxious to spend some time with his brother. The last time they were together was about a week before Lucas was on a plane and off to war. Henry was eager for Lucas to see his new home and how happy he was, married to the love of his life.

Henry could not wait for the week to be over; his big brother will be visiting. It's been over a year since the last time they were together. Lucas called to let Henry know that he will be knocking on his door the day after tomorrow. Henry and Kaccha each took a week's vacation to be able to spend more time with Lucas.

" You are very excited that Lucas will be here the day after tomorrow, I wonder if he is still as handsome as he was when I last saw him."

" Now, now Kaccha you are a happily married women, control your hormones. "

" I know honey I am only teasing you, there is no more room in my heart, because it is filled with love for you. "

They kissed and spent the day making sure everything was in order, they made sure there was enough groceries, they put fresh sheets and blankets on the bed in the guest room. Henry even went so far by checking if there was enough toilet paper. Kaccha laughed when she spotted Henry in the bathroom checking the toilet paper.

" Really Henry. "

" Well yes honey, there is nothing more embarrassing when your visiting friends and you cannot find any toilet paper, been there, done that it is a very awkward situation to say the least. "

" So is there enough paper, mister toilet paper man."

" You are nasty today, I am going to keep my eye on you, mister toilet paper man, I have to admit my love it is a good one. "

" Be careful, there is plenty more where that came from. "

They were both in a playful mood, having fun all day while doing chores. When they were done, they were both sitting on the couch.

" What a wonderful fun day, it is the first time that I have had a blast cleaning the house. You know Kaccha every time I look at you, I still have a hard time believing that such a beautiful woman is my wife, I am truly blessed for having you in my life. I thank god every day."

" The same for me honey, I love you more than yesterday but less than tomorrow, that's how much I love you and always will. You know Henry, my misfortune that night was not all bad after all we met that night, I know there could have been a million better circumstances for us to meet, but here we are today, in love and joyfully married. "

" With all the roadblocks and all the hiccups, we had to go through made us stronger. Nothing will stop us now. We are now on the highway of love, no detours, no exits, keep going forward and never look back. "

The day before Lucas arrived, Henry was in overdrive, bouncing on the wall. Tomorrow could not come soon enough for Henry. After dinner they watched a little bit of tv and off to bed. Henry was really looking forward to waking up and start a new day while waiting for his guests to arrive, the day of Lucas arrival, Henry and Kaccha were putting away the dishes from lunch, when there was a knock on the door. Henry shouted.

" Come in Lucas, I know it is you, I can recognize your knock and you never use the doorbell."

Lucas entered the house with his girlfriend right behind him. The two brothers embraced.

" So happy to see you bro, I missed you. "

" Likewise, my dear brother, not a day went by without my worrying about you I am so glad that you are here. "

" Henry, I want to introduce you the girl that is guilty of stealing my heart, Sandra, I want you to meet Henry."

" It is a pleasure meeting you Henry, I feel as if I have known you for years. Lucas talks about you all the time. We have two topics to talk about life in general and Henry."

" Nice to meet you too, you are way too beautiful to be with a guy like Lucas."

" Lucas warned me that you would have loving words for him. "

" Sandra, I want you to meet my beautiful and loving wife Kaccha "

Sandra walked over to Kaccha and gave her a big hug.

" Such a pleasure to finally having the chance to meet you. "

" Thank you, Sandra it is also a pleasure meeting you."

" Come here Kaccha your more beautiful since the last time I saw you. Henry is a lucky guy."

Kaccha walked over to Lucas and gave him a big hug.

" Please sit down, I will get us something to drink. Henry and Lucas, a beer, yes and you Sandra a beer also.

" Yes"

Kaccha came back in the living room with four beers after lifting their beers and gently nugging each other's beer. They sat down.

" Mom told me about all the headaches and trouble you guys had to go through to finally be here today as a married couple. I am so sorry that I was not able to attend your wedding."

" that's ok you did us a favor."

" What do you mean a favor? "

" We saved a ton of money on food and booze."

" Mom showed me the photos, a nice little wedding."

Lucas walked over to Henry,

" Why you. "

He punched Henry a few times on the shoulders and made his way back to the couch he said.

" You see Sandra, why do you think that I have a mental problem, I had to endure him for way too many years. Were you able to locate your sister to let her know about the wedding? "

" No, I was not able to contact my sister, I have no clue where she is and thanks for introducing us to Sandra, did you count your blessings that you were able to find someone to love that ugly mug of yours? Where and when did you guys meet?"

" I met her four months ago in a bar on the base. She is a combat medic. She is a sweetheart. You cannot imagine how excited I was when she said yes to a dance. Like the song says. Famous first words. And the rest is history. "

" Is that true Sandra how many times did he bug you for a dance before you said yes? "

" you're on a roll little brother, I cannot find the words to describe how I feel to see both of you so happy."

" First of all, now I am not Sandra anymore I am her. Boy how quickly things change, I guess the fireworks in our relationship are gone and to answer your question Henry he was the only man in the bar, and I wanted to dance. "

" I am sorry honey, you know I did not mean anything by saying the word her, it's a common phrase that we men use right Henry? "

" Really I am a man, and I was not aware of that phrase. "

" You see Mr. phrase; Henry is a real gentleman. "

Don't you start, you will be playing right in the hands of that goofball that I used to call a brother."

" No seriously, it was only my second night on the base when I decided to go for a drink and meet new friends, then I ran into this bozzo here. There was something about him that captivated me, instant attraction, his eyes it was his soft caring eyes that were glued to me. The kindness in his voice. He did not even have time to finish the question, would you like to, and I said yes and here we are."

" Lucas what about the secretary at the doctor's office, you know the one you said it was meant to be?"

" Like I said the last time that we talked before my leaving for Afghanistan I told you that I called her a few times, and it did not click. It is a good thing it gave me the chance to meet and love my little angel here."

" Sorry Lucas, to ask you such a silly question and not remembering you telling me it did not click between you and the secretary."

" that's ok bro. No harm done, I told Sandra about the secretary."

" Honey you are improving; I am not a her anymore. "

" Very funny and Henry wipe that smirk off your face. "

They enjoyed a good dinner and talked until the wee hours of the night. The next morning everybody slept in which was great, Henry woke up, he looked at the clock on the night table wow ten o'clock.

" Wake up honey it's ten o'clock, I cannot remember the last time I slept this late."

Kaccha looks at Henry

" Is it really ten o'clock? "

They could hear some noise in the kitchen, Sandra was making coffee.

" I took the liberty of making some coffee is that ok? Your brother is in the washroom."

" Thank you for taking care of the coffee, now that we are all up and ready to tackle the day, I will start breakfast."

" Your welcome Henry."

Lucas came out of the bathroom.

" Man, what a refreshing shower, in Afghanistan if you were in the field, you could go a few days without a shower and a hot meal, so Henry you volunteered to cook breakfast. Make it fast I am hungry. Good morning Kaccha. "

" You will have to wait like everybody else for breakfast to be ready."

Kaccha walked into the kitchen

" Good morning, everyone."

" Good morning Kaccha."

Henry inquired.

" Did you guys sleep well?

" Yes, we did. We slept like two babies in a cradle."

" Slept like babies did you change your diaper, because there is a foul smell in the house this morning."

" Funny little brother. I did change my diaper; I was not sure where to put my soiled diaper and then I found your hiding place for your soiled diapers. "

" Ok guys enough talk about dirty diapers, we are cooking breakfast for god's sake, now you two behave or no breakfast."

" Kaccha, do you agree when they say men never grow up. We have the proof. Listen to them, two kids talking about soiled diapers."

Henry and Lucas responded

" Yes, mommy we will behave, after breakfast can you bring us to the park so we can go play with the other kids."

Kaccha and Sandra rolled their eyes. After a hearty breakfast they remained sitting at the kitchen table enjoying a cup of coffee. Lucas wanted to know what was on the agenda for the day. Henry responded

" I do not know guys what do you want to do today? Lucas for how long are you staying? A month, I hope.

" We are here for a few more days and then it's off to go visit her parents, I am a little nervous, I have yet to meet them, then a week's vacation just the two of us and then back on duty."

" Again, at fort bragg the both of you? "

"Yes, Sandra requested to be transferred to my unit and it was approved."

" You signed up for five years right, Do you know if you will have to go for another tour of duty in Afghanistan? "

" No but I decided when my five years are up, I will stay in the military, making it a career, the same for Sandra, the good thing with the two of us being in the same unit where I go, she goes. "

" That means you will go back to war."

" Well, Kaccha, like the diaper, it depends, some soldiers are in the military twenty, thirty years and never have to experience combat. Enough talk about the army so what are we doing today?"

" Honey, you had to use the word diaper, what's up with that?"

Henry and Lucas started laughing and Lucas said.

" That's for mocking us about the diapers, I might find a way to insert the word diaper in our conversations today. "

Sandra replied.

" Kids you can't live with them, and you cannot shoot them. "

Henry paid back Lucas; the money used to go to India

They spent the day shopping, took in a movie, a long stroll in the park, dinner in a fancy restaurant. The next day, the final day of Lucas and Sandra's visit it was more laid back and out for dinner. Things did not go according to plan. All four were enjoying drinks before dinner, when two couples chose to sit at the table next to them. One of the men could not take his eyes off Kaccha and said.

" Hey, you by looking at you, I know that you are a military guy, aren't you trained to do combat against her kind and not bring them to our homeland? What's with the red dot on her forehead? Is she a suicide bomber, you press the red dot, and she explodes?"

Lucas immediately looked at him and said.

" What do you mean her kind?"

" You know what I am talking about, did you bring her over because she is good in bed? "

Lucas was about to get up when Sandra held him back.

" But honey did you hear what he said?"

" I did let's go before you do something foolish."

All that time Henry was staring at the man and not uttering a word. Lucas looked at Henry and he knew Henry was not going to let that man get away for what he said. All four at the next table were laughing, when Henry approached him.

" You are going to apologize to my wife for what you said."

" Your wife, hey a leprechaun, where is my pot of gold or with a white beard papa smurf. Where do you come from with that accent? They opened the flood gates at the border and look who crawled in. You should be grateful and buy me a beer for letting you stay in my country."

" You know what, the only thing that I regret being a soldier is risking my life to protect pricks like you."

" Who are calling a prick jarhead?"

The restaurant owner approached the four who had just come in and causing the disturbance, he advised all four to leave his restaurant. All four complied but the man had something to say to the owner of the restaurant.

" I was under the assumption that this restaurant was a good clean high-class restaurant, I was wrong. You let people like her in your joint no wonder it stinks in here. Let's go. "

The restaurant owner escorted them to the door and came over to apologize to Kaccha for what the man said.

" Very nice of you to apologize sir, but you did not do anything wrong, you cannot control who comes in your restaurant. It is ok I have learned to ignore that type of person, I will not stoop to his level, ignorant asshole. "

" My little brother has the right to marry the women he loves no matter where she comes from."

" Of course, I hope you can still enjoy your meal, is there something a can do for you? "

Kaccha responded.

" No and thank you for asking, everything is fine. "

The owner walked away but Henry was still flustered about the whole thing. With help from Lucas. He finally calmed down and was able to enjoy his dinner.

" Henry this is the first time that I see such a mean look on your face."

" Well Lucas when it comes to Kaccha I will stop at nothing to protect her. I made her a promise on our wedding day, nobody or anything will never come between us, and I intend to keep that promise at all cost. "

" The day I went to retrieve my belongings. My landlord was causing problems he was really arrogant. Henry punched him in the face."

" No way, you nailed her landlord. I wish I could have been there to witness my little brother punch a man in the face, good for you. Kaccha, I know that Henry will keep his promise."

" I know Henry will keep his promise to always be with me no matter what."

After dinner, they enjoyed a few drinks at a local bar before going home. The remainder of the evening was quiet and pleasant, listening to music while having a few more drinks before going to bed.

The next day after tearful goodbyes and hugs galore. Lucas and Sandra were on their way to meet Sandra's parents. Henry was sad to see them go and wondered when would be the next time, he would enjoy their company. Everything was going great for Henry and Kaccha, good jobs, they purchased their first home, they attended social gatherings, go to dinner in fancy restaurants.

The love between the two grew with every passing day. Life was wonderful but Henry had a longing to find his sister, wanting to know if she was ok, if she was living the good life. Wanting to know was nitpicking at his heart every day. Kaccha understood his feelings, she was feeling the same way about her mom. She missed her mom and couldn't care less about her father.

She was able to find her parents new phone number. She tried calling her mom, her dad answered the phone and refused to let Kaccha speak to her mother. In Arabic he said

" Never call here again, you are no daughter of mine, if you call again to talk to your mother, you made your mother cry for many days if you call and talk to your mother, I punish her because she talks to you. Family now disgraced because of you. Nobody want to be friends with us for what you did, shameful. Understood. You have new phone number. Your mother call to give your number, yes? "

" No using my computer, I was able to find your number and for not calling again. Understood I will never call again."

Henry was feeling guilty living the good life and not knowing the kind of life his sister was living. Maybe she needed help and no one to help her. At Christmas time when mom, dad, Lucas, Sandra, Julie, and Nicole came to visit.

He would say in the back of his mind, the family is not complete, his sister was not with the family, but he was always happy celebrating the holidays with his siblings. Kaccha would look at Henry and say.

" I can see the pain in your face Henry, and I do not like it."

Kaccha suggested that he should go to South Africa and try to locate his sister, it would put his mind at ease to know she was doing well, Henry pondered the idea of going for a couple of weeks before making a decision to go to South Africa to find his sister. One day when he came home from work. He said to Kaccha.

" Kaccha I will go to South Africa and find my sister Louane, not knowing how she is, is killing me, I applied for a two-week vacation starting Monday, it was approved. So, I have four days to get ready."

" I wish I could go with you but things at work are crazy, we can hardly keep up with the demands from chemical companies. "

" No worries, honey no sense of you wasting your vacation time to come with me, I will be just fine by myself. I will accomplish more alone.

The following day Henry booked his flight to South Africa, checked his passport. He would be leaving Sunday morning for his eighteen-hour flight to his destination. He advised his mom and dad of his plans, provided several contact numbers in case of an emergency.

Kaccha drove him to the airport, little did he know it would be the last time he would see Kaccha able to stand up and talk to him. The contact numbers would be useless to contact Henry.

" I love you Henry be careful, I will miss you, I hope you can find your sister. When you come back, I will be right here waiting for you. I love you."

They hugged, kissed, Kaccha waited until she could no longer see Henry. Henry had tears in his eyes, he was sad to leave Kaccha, but happy at the prospect of finding his sister. It would be the last time, that Kaccha would talk face to face with Henry. Before leaving he called his mom and dad to make sure they had the right contact numbers to reach him.

" It is vital, that you remember the contact numbers that I gave you. The numbers are essential to be able to stay in touch. "

The contact numbers provided by Henry would be useless. The hospital called the numbers, and they were not able to reach him.

CHAPTER 7

When his flight landed Henry called Kaccha to let her know that although it was a long flight it went smoothly, and he was going to his hotel to get some sleep.

The conversation would be the last between Kaccha and Henry. There is a time difference between the two countries, South Africa time his six hours ahead from the United States.

Henry's day was well under way when the alarm clock beside the bed, made Kaccha jump out of bed and get ready for work. Kaccha worked on the second floor of the building. She rarely took the elevator. Her motto was I can exercise while at work going up and down the stairs.

Kaccha always made sure her area of work was always tidy before going home. After a long and busy day, it took Kaccha some extra time to put everything where it was supposed to be. She was eager to go home and talk to Henry. Although the six hours difference Henry will not go to bed until he had spoken to Kaccha.

She looked at her watch it was five forty-five, she should be home by six fifteen. She was in a hurry, so she started trotting down the stairs, she tripped and tumbled down the remaining nine steps, hitting her head on most of the steps and landed head first on the marble floor, she suffered multiple injuries but the most critical one was when she hit the marble floor and split her head wide open.

There were only a few employees remaining in the building. It took close to an hour before she was spotted by an employee going down another set of stairs. She called 911 and ran over to Kaccha. There was a puddle of blood around her head. Kaccha did not move since hitting the floor.

She was unconscious with a very weak pulse. Within fifteen minutes, the paramedics arrived and whisked her away by ambulance to the nearest hospital.

The surgical team at the hospital was ready when the ambulance arrived, they rushed Kaccha to the operation room. The brain surgeon did not waste a minute as soon as all preparations for the surgery where done he was hard at work to try and save Kaccha's life.

Kaccha was on the operating table for six hours. The surgeon did everything he could to try to repair the damage done to her brain, it would take a few more operations in order for the surgeon to complete what needed to be done. Kaccha remained in a coma.

The doctor's prognosis was the longer Kaccha remained in a coma, if she was to wake up, she would be in a vegetable state at best. She suffered irreversible brain damage. Henry waited patiently in his hotel room for a call from Kaccha. He was expecting her call around midnight South Africa time. Henry was exhausted from his day of searching for his sister and dozed off.

Henry did not wake up until morning, he checked his phone for messages, no message from Kaccha. Maybe she called and did not leave a message which it would have been bizarre for her to not leave a message.

Their home phone number did not show in the caller id. This is weird, it was not like her not to call. He tried calling home, no answer the answering machine came on, so he left her a message. He called her cell phone, same thing the call also went to her voicemail.

It was eight am. In South Africa, two am. At home, Kaccha was probably sleeping and did not hear the phone. He kept thinking how strange it was that she did not call. He would not leave his room until he knew why Kaccha did not call.

Henry was hoping as soon as she walked in the house, she was exhausted and hit the sack. He called home again eight am. U.S. time no answer. Tried her cell phone, someone answered.

" Kaccha are you ok?"

" I am sorry this is not Kaccha, who are you? "

" I am her husband, who am I speaking too? "

" Sir you are talking to a nurse at UC San Diego medical center."

" Excuse me you are who from where?"

" I am a nurse, your wife is in our care, she stumbled down the stairs at her work and needed emergency brain surgery. We tried to reach you at home, we tried several numbers that are in her cell phone. We could not reach anyone."

" How is she and when did the accident occur? "

" She is in a coma and in critical condition."

" How come someone from the hospital did not call me. You could have called the numbers in her phone? "

" Like I said sir we tried several times to reach you sir. But the calls would not connect. "

" My cell phone is working fine; I am talking to you with my phone. "

" I do not know sir why the calls did not connect, but like I said your wife is in critical condition and in a coma."

" It might take me several days to get home, it is a seventeen-hour flight, and I am not sure if I can get a ticket tonight or tomorrow. "

" She is at San Diego medical center."

" Thank you see you soon."

Henry was full of guilt for going on a quest to find his sister and leaving Kaccha alone, he called the airline to book a seat on the next available flight to San Diego. The earliest that he could get was for the following afternoon at one o'clock. He called his parents to let them know about the situation and the guilt he was feeling because of leaving her alone.

" Mom I was selfish to leave Kaccha alone and go find my sister. I will never forgive myself."

" Henry listen to me and listen to me good. It is not your fault, now stop that nonsense of feeling guilty or else it's going to drive you crazy. Put that guilty feeling away. You will need all your energy to stay on top of things for Kaccha's sake. Get home as soon as you can, and we will see you at the hospital. Like I said ditch the guilty trip and focus on coming home ok."

" Mom no need for you and dad to make the trip to San Diego, I can keep you posted."

" that's sweet Henry but we will go spend a few days."

" Are you sure mom, how is dad doing, I know he's been feeling under the weather lately? "

" He is doing a lot better."

" Good, don't forget your key for the house and make yourselves at home, my flight is tomorrow at one pm. It's a seventeen-hour flight, so I will see you in two days. I love you both very much mom, I cannot wait to get home. She is at the San Diego medical center."

" We love you too, have a safe flight, see you in a few days. "

Henry also called Lucas to let him know what happened and Kaccha's condition when Lucas answered the phone.

" Hey little brother, have you made any progress in locating your sister? "

" No, I wish I did, Kaccha is in the hospital in a coma, in critical condition. She tripped going down the stairs at work and split her head wide open. "

" No, no, no are you kidding me, where are you now?"

" I am still in South Africa; I fly out tomorrow afternoon. Before calling you, I was talking to mom, she mentioned that dad is feeling better, and they will meet me at the hospital."

" Listen Henry I am at the airport, we are taking a plane in about an hour to go join Sandra's parents in Hawaii but, I need to be there with you. Give me a few minutes and I will call you back."

Sandra inquired.

" What's going on?"

" Kaccha is in a coma and in critical condition after stumbling down the stairs at work."

" Poor her she cannot catch a break. What now? "

" Honey, I need to be there."

" What about our trip to Hawaii to join my mom and dad?"

" I am sure they will understand."

" Can you come for at least maybe a day or two? We have been looking forward to this vacation before our next deployment in the Middle East."

" I know it's breaking my heart not being able to go but, my brother needs me, and it might be the last time I see him before we leave in a couple of weeks, I hope you understand honey. "

" Yes, I do. All right then, it's time to board the plane, see you soon honey. "

Lucas kissed and hugged Sandra, watched her board the plane, wishing he was boarding the plane with her and called Henry

" Henry see you in San Diego."

" Ok. "

" Listen I am going to go join mom and dad at the hospital."

" Ok but what about Sandra and your trip to Hawaii? "

" I will talk to you at the hospital, see you soon."

Lucas turned his attention on getting to San Diego. He was lucky, he was able to book a flight for later that evening, what a relief it was for him to be able to fly to San Diego that night.

Lucas was really anxious to get to the hospital. When his plane landed, he took a taxi to the hospital, his mom and dad were already by Kaccha's bedside. When Lucas entered the room, tears rolled down his cheeks, all three embraced and walked out the room.

" When did you guys get here? "

" Two hours ago."

" When do you think Henry will get here?"

" He should be here in a day or two."

" I wonder how poor Henry is going to react to see her this way, he loves her more than any man can love a woman. We need to be here with him when he enters her room. He is going to need all the support that he can get. Why did this have to happen? They were enjoying the good life, Kaccha and Henry merged their souls together and became only one. Boy it's been a long day for me, mom, dad let's go get something to eat. I hope the food is good I am starving."

With such a big staff at the hospital and countless visitors the cafeteria was open twenty-four hours a day. They made their way to the cafeteria, they sat at a table close to a window. His mother started the conversation by saying.

" Sandra must have been disappointed because you did not go with her to Hawaii. To tell you the truth we were both surprised to see you here. "

" Henry called me right after he finished talking to you, I was at the airport ready to board the plane to Hawaii when he called. Yes, Sandra was not happy about the situation, but she understood the need for me to be here. It is our last vacation before we leave for the middle east."

" It's a shame all of this had to happen. Poor Kaccha everything she had to go through to be with Henry. They were building a comfortable life. They say God works in mysterious ways, I sure would like to know what is so mysterious about this situation, good honest people in love, earning an honest living, why this I will never understand? "

" I know dad, I asked myself the same question why them, I know she is not gone I do not want to be morbid, if she wakes up in a vegetative state, what next? Did either one of you have a chance to talk to a doctor yet?"

" No not yet, when the nurses come and check on Kaccha, they are tight lipped when it comes to wanting information. They all say the same thing, you will have to speak to the doctor."

" I guess mom, they are sworn to secrecy. Why don't we go home and get some rest, tomorrow is going to be a long day. We can wait until Henry's flight lands at the airport no need for us to be at the hospital until Henry arrives so we can relax and get some rest, we will have to be strong for Henry. When the time comes, I will drop you guys at the hospital, and I will go to the airport."

" Yes, we both want to be there. Tomorrow, we need to stay calm and focused on not getting overwhelmed with emotions. We need to be strong for Henry. If we open the floodgates of emotions, we will be swimming in an ocean of emotions and we need to avoid that because we will be drowning in our tears."

" We understand dad it will not be an easy task, but we need to remain calm in order to give Henry all the support he needs. You don't mind my driving your car dad. I have matured since the last time I was behind the wheel of your car. "

" I hope so the last time you drove my car it cost me an arm and a leg in repairs. Remember?"

" How could I forget every week you would talk about how expensive it was to repair my blunder behind the wheel."

" Ok boys let's go home and get some sleep."

The next day, when it was time to go to the airport. Lucas dropped his parents at the hospital and made his way to the airport, after parking the car, he grabbed a coffee, checked the time of arrival for Henry's flight, a forty-five-minute wait. He spotted a small couch, once seated he said.

" Boy this couch is really comfortable; I hope I do not doze off."

Lucas was trying to find a way to greet Henry, he knew it would be a sad moment for both. After a half hour of waiting, Lucas fell asleep. He was awakened by Henry kicking his foot.

" Wake up sleeping beauty."

" Oh my gosh Henry, I am so sorry for falling asleep."

" that's ok when did you get here?"

" Forty-five minutes ago, it is sure nice to see you, I wish it would be under better circumstances. Come here little brother."

Lucas hugged Henry, they were both crying, looked at each other, Lucas picked up Henry's luggage, they silently walked to the car. Not a word was said until they were both in the car.

" You know Lucas, I am really sorry for messing up your vacation, there was no need for you to be here. I should have kept my mouth shut and not call you. "

" Henry, you know as well as I do family comes first. Yes, Sandra was a bit disappointed, but she understands. Not calling me was not a option, I would have been hurt and pissed for not contacting me. Mom and dad are already at the hospital waiting for you."

" How is dad doing, how is he holding up? "

" Dad is feeling better but he is not out of the woods yet. He might need heart surgery. Mom is ok but she is very worried about dad. "

" Lucas I am trying to put on a brave face for both mom and dad as we are getting closer to the hospital my emotions are starting to get the best of me. Did you know, we were planning on taking a two-week Caribbean cruise, make it like sort of our honeymoon. We did not go on a honeymoon when we got married. Kaccha was so looking forward to the trip. The excitement of being on a cruise ship and to be able to finally have our honeymoon. "

Henry was holding back tears, he wanted to be strong for Kaccha and his family, but it was getting very difficult for him to keep his composure.

" Henry, do you want to get something to eat or go home and change before going to the hospital? "

" No thanks I want to go straight to the hospital; I should have been there for her."

" Mom told me you were feeling guilty for leaving her alone, how could you have known something was going to happen. Stop with that guilty crap, you are going to drive yourself crazy, understand."

" Yes, you're right, I am not a psychic. I cannot know what will take place tomorrow. Lucas my hands are starting to shake, I am having a hard time breathing."

" Henry we will be there in a minute, now look at me and listen to the sound of my voice, you are stronger than you think, be brave for Kaccha and mom and dad. Believe me Henry while in Afghanistan I was no stranger to panic attacks. Take a deep breath and release it slowly. We are here Henry. Take a few more deep breaths before we get out of the car. There you go, feel a little better now."

" Yes."

" Good for you, be strong little brother for everyone's sake."

CHAPTER 8

Lucas was driving around the parking lot to find a parking space.

" This is it buddy, we are at the hospital."

After finding a parking spot Lucas and Henry made their way to the hospital entrance. Lucas was keeping a close eye on Henry.

" Are you ok buddy?"

" What floor is she on? "

" Floor seven, I know Henry I am not in your shoes, but be strong for mom, dad and Kaccha. I know how you feel, I lost friends on the battlefield. Kaccha will need you. "

Lucas called his mom to let her know, that they are on their way upstairs.

" Henry, do you need a moment before we take the elevator? "

" No, I am ok, I will try my best to keep my composure."

Lucas pressed the elevator button; in a few moments Henry will get his first glimpse of Kaccha in her hospital bed. His parents were waiting at the elevator, when the door opened and Henry saw his parents, he gave them a big hug. All four were now crying. They stayed put for a few minutes to collect themselves. When they reached the threshold of Kaccha's room. Henry froze he could not go any further.

" I can't enter the room and see her lying in bed, not moving and all the things wired to her. I am so nervous I think I am going to throw up."

" Henry remember our talk in the car, you need to go in if you don't go in right now, you might never to be able to go in, we do not want that. Kaccha needs you by her side. Now take a few deep breaths and let's go in."

His mom took him by the hand, they stepped in the room. Henry's eyes where closed, when he reached the side of the bed, he opened his eyes. He stood there in shock for a few minutes before he was able to utter a few words, tears flowing down his cheeks. He took Kaccha's hand.

" Kaccha, Kaccha, Kaccha no, no. Please come back to me, please, please, please, please I love you so much, please come back to me, I can't live without you, please I need you to come back to me. Please. "

By then Henry was on his knees, sobbing out of control, it was breaking their heart to see him on his knees sobbing. Lucas grabbed him by the hand.

" Come on little brother, let's go for a walk."

Henry stood up, followed Lucas in the hallway. Lucas gave him a big hug.

" It's ok to cry. Believe me I feel your pain. I hate seeing you like this. Let's go to the cafeteria and get some food in your stomach. When was the last time you had something to eat?"

" A snack on the plane."

" Mom, dad, we will be back in a few minutes, need something from the cafeteria?"

" No, we are fine for the moment, thank you for asking."

" Ok dad, we will be back in a few minutes."

" Take your time son, no need to rush, we are not going anywhere."

Once in the cafeteria they were both holding back their tears. They grabbed a tray.

" Come on Henry let's go see what is on the menu today."

The cafeteria was almost empty, Lucas was able to find a small table for two.

" Dig in, for hospital food, the roast beef is good, not delicious but good."

" Do you know that cows are sacred in India, that's why we do not have any beef products in the house."

" Come on Henry eat, you need your strength, we do not want to witness you faint because of a lack of food and in need of medical attention, we also worry about you, so do not make it worse by not eating is that what you want for us to watch you crumble in front of our eyes? Listen to your big brother. I want you to gulp down all the food in your plate."

" Ok enough with the sermon, look I am eating, I will do everything in my power to stay strong and positive happy now."

" I know you are upset but don't gripe at me, I am only trying to help and support you, so you can support yourself."

" If you're that worried how come you could not stay awake at the airport when people worry, they are too nervous to sleep?"

" You know I am worried, it was a long day, up early this morning."

" I was pulling your leg; I know you care and want the best for me. You are intervening in the school yard that day to help me was the start of an unbreakable bond between us that will never be broken. I am so lucky and blessed to have you in my life big brother, you are always able to push me forward when I need it. I love you man."

" I know, and good you still have your sense of humor, are you ready to go back upstairs?

" Yes, this time I will try to keep my composure and not cry like a lunatic."

Before entering the room, Henry paced the floor in the hallway for a few minutes, taking deep breaths, nodded his head to indicate he was ready to go in. The doctor was in the room. Two nurses were in the process of washing Kaccha. The doctor introduced himself to Henry. They shook hands

" Hi, I am doctor Applebee are you her husband?"

" Yes, I am, how is she doctor?"

They both retreated in the hallway for more privacy.

" She is as well as she can be under the circumstances. She suffered irreversible brain damage. Her back is bruised. We try to keep her as comfortable as we can."

" Irreversible brain damage."

" Yes, sir that means when she wakes up if she does wake up. She will be in a vegetative state. Do you know what that means?"

" There is nothing else you can do to help her."

" We did everything we could to help her. I am so sorry sir to be the bearer of bad news."

" No need to apologize doctor, I thank you from the bottom of my heart for everything you are doing for my wife."

" You're welcome, I have to go finish my rounds, you can talk to her, she can hear everything that is going on around her. Also, sir I advised the front desk that you can stay as long as you want and to get you a comfortable chair. Talk to you in the morning."

As Henry watched the doctor walk away, he was trying to take it all in. The shock that Kaccha is in a vegetative state for the rest of her life. When Henry walked back in the room is mom said.

" He told you the same grim news that he told us."

" Yes, he did."

Henry walked to Kaccha's bedside, took a chair, sat down as close as possible to her head.

" The doctor told me she can ear and understand me when I talk to her, so I am not budging from this chair until she wakes up. You guys can go home because I am not going anywhere. Mom, dad I do not want you guys to get to tired, especially you dad."

" I am fine, why is everyone so worried about me I am fit as a fiddle."

" Yes, a fiddle that needs some tuning."

" Very funny Lucas, I am stronger than you think."

" Henry is right go home get some rest, I will stay a little longer. See you guys later."

" Honey my love, I am here for you, I will not leave your bedside until you get better. Lucas is with me today. So, honey wherever you are please come back. I will be here waiting for you. So please, please, please come back to me please."

Henry looked at Lucas again both men were holding back tears. The room was silent. Henry was silently praying, Lucas was trying to absorb the situation and thinking he will be leaving in a few days to go meet Sandra and then go back to the army base. His worst dilemma, in a few weeks he will be deployed to the middle east. He hated the fact that he was going to be so far away when Henry needed him the most.

" Lucas when are leaving for your next deployment? "

" In about two weeks."

" When are you supposed to report to basecamp?"

" In six days."

" In six days, wow you won't have much time to enjoy Hawaii. Go spend some time in paradise with Sandra. I am sure she will be happy to see you. "

" I called her when you were talking to the doctor, she sends her regards and all her positive vibes your way."

" that's very kind of her. What day is she expecting you to join her?"

" I told her in a few days."

" Lucas you get your ass on a plane tomorrow go join your girlfriend and have fun."

" Mom and dad are leaving the day after tomorrow, so I am leaving the day after tomorrow. We hate to leave you in your time of need, but we have no choice. Dad needs to see his doctor and you know about my situation."

" I will be fine, it will be sad to see all of you go, I will survive, I will keep you guys posted. Mom and dad please go home and get some rest."

" Ok we will go, see you in the morning."

" I will stay a little while longer."

Lucas phone rings.

" Hello, hey hi you two, ... Yes, Henry is by her bedside.... The prognosis is not good.... what's that.... yes, mom and dad and myself we are leaving the day after tomorrow......she is still in a coma and will be bedridden for the rest of her life....in a vegetative state......ok thanks for calling....

yes I will....love you too. Julie and Nicole send you their best regards, they are so sorry they cannot be here. They will pray for you."

" Nice of them to call"

A nurse walked in the room, to check on Kaccha, scribbled a few notes on a piece of paper.

" I will be back in two hours to check on her again."

" Thank you."

" You are welcome."

" Come Henry lets go get something to eat. "

" Yes, good idea, Kaccha, I will be back in few minutes. I am going with Lucas to get something to eat, see you soon. "

They made their way to the cafeteria, once seated with their meal. Lucas broke the silence with a question.

" You know Henry we all feel guilty for leaving, are you sure that you will be able to cope by yourself? "

" Well to answer your question, I am not sure, but I will try my very best, I have to be strong and put my feelings aside and really focus on what needs to be done for Kaccha. Her needs will give me strength to do what needs to be done. The stronger I am the more I will be able to help Kaccha. I will draw my strength from Kaccha. "

" Good I am happy to hear that, you know you will be surprised when needed we always find that dormant inner strength that we all have. You will be surprised how much energy you can draw from what we call our fifth gear that we keep in reserve until needed. "

" Do not worry, I will find this fifth gear and put it in overdrive for as long as I need it for Kaccha sake. The focus is on her, not on me. "

After finishing their meal, they made their way to Kaccha's room. Lucas stayed with Henry for another hour and then made his way home.

" Well Henry I think I am going to hit the road. I will see you in the morning. Take care bro, don't forget if things change do not hesitate to call. Goodnight."

" Goodnight and thanks for everything."

" Always."

" How are you going to get home? You do not have your car."

" I will take a taxi see you in the morning."

" Here Lucas money for the taxi. "

" Come on Henry don't offer me money, do you want to insult me? You need it more than I do. See you in the morning. "

Henry was now alone in the room with Kaccha. He kept staring at the bed. Closed his eyes hoping it was only a nightmare. Sitting in the chair next to the bed, now alone reality started to kick in. He whispered a few words to Kaccha, a few moments later he was able to fall asleep. He was awakened by the nurse in the room.

" Sorry sir I tried to be as quiet as possible."

" No worries and thank you for the good service. No changes in her condition?"

" I am afraid not sir, she is stable, not feeling any pain, the doctor will come by in the morning, if you need anything sir the nurse's desk is right down the hall, have a goodnight, sir."

Early the next morning, as promised, his parents and brother were at the hospital. Henry called the school board for a prolonged leave of absence.

" No changes? "

" No mom no changes."

" Come with me little brother lest go get some breakfast."

Sitting at a table eating breakfast, Henry needed to talk about his feelings, he was afraid and did not know what to do.

" Lucas can I confide in you? I really need to talk about things. You know you are the person next to Kaccha that I cherish the most in this whole wide world. "

" What's on your mind little buddy? If you need to empty your basket of thoughts and fears do not hold back, I can feel the apprehension in your voice. I am listening. "

" Last night alone in the room with Kaccha, reality hit me like a knockout punch. When you, mom and dad were with me at hospital, I did not grasp the reality of the situation, I now realize our lives are over, we will never be a happy couple again. I know someone, like another doctor will advise doctor Applebee to pull the plug to stop her suffering and let her sleep-in peace, I might be selfish, but I will never make that decision, I can't, I will bring her home and care for her myself, no matter the cost. I intend to keep my promise in sickness and in health and until death do us part and that's what I intend to do."

While talking to Lucas, Henry could not hold back his tears. Lucas was also very emotional.

" Henry, you know I will never tell you what to do, because if I was in your shoes, I do not know what I would do. One thing that I can tell you, nobody can make that decision but you. Do not let anyone influence you about changing your mind. If you, do you will regret making that decision for the rest of your life. "

" You probably think that I am selfish thinking this way."

" No, I am not, let me put it this way, if Kaccha could talk maybe she could tell you yes or no. But you do not know that. Maybe Kaccha would still have the will to live or to turn off the lights for good. So, in my opinion it would be her decision to make not yours."

" Your right, it never dawned on me that it would be her decision not mind. If I tell the doctor to let her go, we would be committing a legal murder. "

" Now Henry you have a big responsibly on your shoulders, it will be very expensive and time consuming. You will have a lot of planning and decisions to make and do not look to far ahead, take it one day at a time, otherwise you might end up climbing the walls if you know what I mean. Don't forget, I am only a phone call away. "

" Thanks, you were able to clear a path for me to follow."

" Remember Henry, it is not something, I told you to do, it's only my opinion, ready to go back upstairs?"

" Yes, I know. "

The door of her room was closed, mom and dad were standing in the hallway. Henry inquired.

" What's going on, why is the door closed?"

" The doctor is doing a few more tests this morning, that's why the door is closed."

" What kind of test mom, did the doctor say anything?"

" No all he said for us to leave the room for thirty minutes, a few tests needed to be done. "

" How long have you been waiting to go back in?"

" Twenty minutes, the doctor should be out soon."

While waiting for the doctor to exit the room, Lucas noticed how pale his father was.

" Dad are you alright, have you noticed how pale you are?"

" No not really, it could be the ceiling lights that makes my skin look pale."

" I don't think so honey, it can't be the lights look at us. Do we look pale to you?"

" Mom, dad go home, get some rest, your flight is tomorrow, you have a long day ahead of you. I am ok Lucas is with me."

" Henry is right, mom and dad go home."

" We only got here about an hour ago. "

" I know mom I am blessed that you are both here with me. I love you both and I want to be blessed for many years, to come."

" We will not be able to come by before our flight tomorrow I want to hear what the doctor as to say and then we will go."

The doctor stepped out of the room, all four were anxious to know if there was any improvement in Kaccha's condition.

" We did a few tests to give me a better understanding on what she can feel and not feel, like pinching for example. She can feel pain, she slightly moved her fingers and the same thing for her toes. I pulled a strand of her hair, and I noticed a little bit of movement from her lips. Mind you this could change tomorrow and show no movement and no change in her condition. We hope to see some improvement in the coming week. We will keep monitoring her every two hours, we keep hoping for the best. We will see what tomorrow brings, take care folks, I have to finish my morning rounds. "

" At least she is showing signs of life, shc can feel things. That's a big improvement don't you think?"

" Hold on Henry, we are all wishing for her to recover, I do not want to be pessimistic, please do not put the wagon in front of the horse. He said there was no changes in her condition and her reactions when touched can change by tomorrow."

" Yes, Henry Lucas is right, take one day at a time, or else you will get high hopes and you might crash and burn. I do the same for your father, when he is ill, I focus only one day at a time."

" Henry, do you remember what we talked about while having breakfast? "

" I heard what you said mom, I had a good discussion with Lucas about the same subject. Do no worry I will take things good or bad one day at a time. I promise, you know I never break a promise. Now you two go home."

Lucas spent the remainder of the day at the hospital with Henry. When it came time for Lucas to leave, they embraced, said their goodbyes. Henry watched Lucas wait for the elevator, he wondered when will be the next time he would see his brother again.

" I am on my own."

A lone wolf surrounded by strangers. He made himself comfortable in the big chair provided by the hospital. Henry was exhausted from a lack of sleep. He closed his eyes and fell asleep. When the nurses made their rounds every two hours, they made sure not to make any noise to wake up Henry. The next morning one of the nurses brought Henry some breakfast.

" Here sir this is for you. "

" Thank you, there was no need for you to take the time and trouble to get me some breakfast."

" No trouble at all sir. I was getting my morning coffee; I knew you would be hungry. You are a very sweet and devoted man. Kaccha is lucky to have such a loving husband. The doctor will come to examine your wife in about an hour in the meantime if you need anything do not hesitate to ask."

" Kaccha is lucky to have such caring people looking after her. Again, thank you for the breakfast. It will hit the spot. Oh, I much do I owe you?"

" A smile. "

Henry smiled with a big grin from ear to ear.

" Now that's a smile thank you."

Lucas called Henry to let him know, all three were on their way to the airport. The nurse walked out of the room, Henry was counting his blessings that Kaccha was well taken care of, at least it was one less thing he needed to worry about. Finished with his breakfast, Henry positioned himself so that he could talk to Kaccha.

" I know you can hear me my darling. I love you more and more each day. My heart keeps growing each day with the love I have for you, my heart is now the size of my chest, it will keep expanding every day. You are the love of my life; I wrote you a little poem I hope you like it. "

" Kaccha my love, please be with me always, my little dove, love you more and more every day, my one and only girl, I love you so deeply, my shining pearl, you will always be my sweetie, that I know it is so true, for there is no one else, now I am feeling blue, I am all by myself, my heart beats just for you, no matter what happens, I am hanging on without a clue, everyday my love deepens, you are the one and only one for me. "

" So, what do you think? Not bad for a beginner. "

Henry would spend day and night by Kaccha's bedside. Each day Henry would write a poem for Kaccha. He would only leave her bedside to go home to change clothes, take a shower and get something to eat at the hospital cafeteria.

One morning the doctor advised him that he should take a break go home for a good night sleep. Henry refused to leave her side just in case she would wake up, he wanted to be the first person she would see when she opened her eyes.

" You know Henry if she does wake up there is a chance that she might not recognize you."

" I know but I do not want to leave her bedside."

When Lucas and Sandra reported for duty, Lucas was promoted to the rank of sergeant. He was no longer going to Saudi Arabia. He was headed back to Afghanistan for a second tour of duty. Again, Lucas requested that Sandra be transferred to his new unit. It was approved.

They would be leaving for Afghanistan in three weeks' time. Lucas called his folks to let them know. They congratulated him on his promotion and to be extra careful and not take unnecessary chances. Lucas called Henry to tell him the news and inquire about Kaccha.

" Hello."

" Henry it's Lucas how are you holding up buddy, any changes in Kaccha's condition?"

" No changes on Kaccha's condition and me well let's just say I am hanging on by a thread."

" Keep hanging on to that thread Henry, I also called to let you know I was promoted to sergeant and instead of deploying to Saudi Arabia, I am going back to Afghanistan for a second tour of duty. Sandra is coming along with me, when we get back, we will get married, I want you to be my best man."

"That's great, I am happy and nervous for both of you and congratulations on your promotion, that means you will be leading men into battle. So please come back in one piece. I will be honored to be your best man.

I assume you called mom and dad to let them know your change of plans."

" Yes, I did that's all the time I have, I have to go, it's a one-year tour we leave in three weeks. See you when I get back little brother, I love you man."

One morning while he was reading a poem to Kaccha her eyes blinked. Henry ran to go get the nurse.

" Come quickly Kaccha, her eyes blinked while I was reciting a poem in her ear."

Henry was right when the nurse entered the room Kaccha's eyes where half opened. She hurried to the front desk.

" Page Dr. Applebee asap, Kaccha is waking up."

The nurse hurried back to the room. When the doctor arrived, Kaccha's eyes where still half open.

" Kaccha I am Dr. Applebee, your doctor, I know you can hear me, please open those gorgeous blue eyes for me."

Kaccha did the opposite she closed her eyes. The doctor reassured Henry that it was perfectly normal. It meant that she was slowly waking up. It's a good sign, he was confident within the next few days Kaccha will no longer be in a coma. Henry was elated by the prospect of Kaccha finally waking up from her coma.

Several days went by with no other movement of her eyes was detected. Henry's balloon was deflating a little every day, until one morning Kaccha opened her eyes. Kaccha was finally awake. Henry ran to the nurse's aid station.

" Come and see Kaccha is awake, finally she is awake, hurry come and see for yourselves. "

The nurse ran to the room and paged Dr. Applebee. Henry was beside her bed trying to communicate with her when the doctor entered the room.

" Look doctor she is awake, it's wonderful, I am so happy, do you think she is now awake for good doctor, no more coma?"

" We will have to wait and see, nurse can you come here for a minute? Henry can you please step out of the room for a few minutes? "

" But why doctor she is awake?"

" I am very well aware that she is awake, I need you to step out for a moment please. "

Henry was waiting in the hallway when a man approached him.

" Excuse me sir my name is James, is it your wife in the room? The reason I am asking is that my wife was rushed here last night because of a drive by shooting. She was walking along on the sidewalk with her friend and a passing car opened fire for no reason at all. Her friend collapsed on the sidewalk dead; my wife was critically wounded with two bullets to the head. Is this a good hospital for brain injuries?"

" No worries there my friend, very good doctors, friendly staff, my name is Henry, my wife was in a coma, this morning she opened her eyes. The doctor asked me to step out of the room for a few minutes, I do not know why?"

" Thanks a million sir for the information, you put my mind at ease knowing that my wife will be well taken care of, my wife is in room 705. Have you seen the annoying lady that walks in the hallway stating, there is a cure for cancer, they found a plant that would cure all cancers, but the government keeps it a secret because they are making money with the pharmaceutical companies. That she knows for a fact, she has proof. Here she comes."

" It's the first time that she is headed this way, usually she goes in the opposite direction. "

Every day the lady would come by and tell the same story over and over, Henry and James tried to avoid her but for some reason she was always able to find them. The lady was in the hospital for a number of health issues and would be at the hospital for many weeks to come. When the doctor stepped out of the room, he explained to Henry that yes Kaccha was out of her coma and like predicted she is a vegetative state.

" Henry when I entered the room, you were trying to communicate with Kaccha. I am sorry to tell you communication with Kaccha is impossible, she is awake with no signs of awareness. For the moment she will not respond to what is happening around her. There are more symptoms that I need to discuss with you later. "

" Ok doctor talk to you soon."

Henry was feeling a sigh of relief, no more worries about her not waking up from her coma. Henry called his parents to let them know that Kaccha was awake. They were very happy about the news; his mom will try to reach Lucas to let him know.

" That's terrific news Henry, I am so happy and relieved to hear that she is finally out of her coma. Your father on the other hand his health is not that great. I am very worried about him. The doctor prescribed him some new medication. The doctor will also monitor his heart."

" Geezz mom sorry to hear that, you will keep me posted on any changes in his health, good or bad. Is Lucas aware of all this?"

" I could not reach him; he will be back tomorrow from a training session before he goes back to Afghanistan. "

" Ok mom give my love to dad and tell him to get better asap and do not forget keep me posted please. Love you mom."

" Love you son, thanks for calling."

Henry and James became good friends, every day they would meet in the cafeteria for coffee, have long chats in the hallway. Henry would go home every second day to take a shower and a change of clothes.

One day when Henry went home for a shower and a change of clothes, he noticed that someone left him a message on his answering machine the message was from the school board, wanting to know when Henry would return to work.

The deal was during his absence, Henry was receiving full pay in exchange when Henry would go back to work, he would be receiving two thirds of his salary until his debt was paid in full to the school board. The president of the school board wanted to let Henry know; his leave of absence would finish in three weeks and to make sure that Henry returned to work when his leave of absence was over.

" I have to go back to work in three weeks, what about you James?"

" Me at the moment I am jobless, I have four months of employment insurance before I need to find a job, by then I hope my wife will be well enough for me to go back to work."

One afternoon the doctor approached Henry to discuss the possibility of Kaccha going home or to a long-term medical facility which was an hour away from the hospital. Henry would have to think about options.

His house is twenty minutes away from the hospital and work is thirty minutes from the hospital, it would take him an hour and a half of driving one way to get to the long-term facility which meant a three-hour commute. No way he would be able to visit Kaccha after work. He would only see her during weekends, which is not acceptable, Kaccha will be going home.

Henry spotted James in the hallway leaning against the wall, Henry walked towards him. James was crying.

" Henry my wife is gone, the nurse went to check on her, early this morning, Nancy was dead. The doctor did advise me the chances of her making a recovery where very slim. I was on my way to the hospital when I received the call. Henry, I did not get a chance to tell Nancy a final goodbye. She is gone to heaven knowing, I was not there beside her, she passed away alone in a hospital room. She was alone when she died, poor Nancy she was alone, alone in her room Henry, alone, I should have been beside her when she passed away."

" I am so sorry for your lost my dear friend, but she is now in a better place. Your grief about her being alone when she passed away. She knew you were trying your best to be by her side every day."

" I did not get to say goodbye."

" The reason she did not wait for you before taking her final breath. She wanted to spare you the pain of witnessing her final moments on this earth. She was also aware every day before leaving you said goodbye. She knew that it might be your final goodbye to her. So, you did say your final goodbye."

" You really think so Henry."

" Yes, I do, her spirit would relay your message to her brain. You would be amazed the information that you can find on the internet regarding brain injuries and communicating with spirits. If you have a chance to read up on the subjects, believe me it will do you a lot of good and probably help you, getting rid of your guilty trip. "

" Do you believe in all that stuff about spirits, ghost and so on?"

" Well, James my friend, with the new technology nowadays, they can debunk almost everything."

" They will be transferring Nancy to the morgue in a few minutes, I guess this is goodbye my friend, talking to you on a daily basis really helped me to cope. Can we stay in touch?"

" Absolutely, I did not get a chance to know Nancy but from what you told me. She was a very good person with a big heart. Here's my number, call me to let me know when and where her funeral will be held, and I will be there."

" Thanks Henry, I really appreciate that, I will definitely give you a call for sure and good luck with that annoying lady."

They shook hands and James was on his way to the morgue Henry watched him walk away. Poor guy he was hoping that things could change, and his wife would make a miraculous recovery.

The following day James contacted Henry to let him know the details on where and when the funeral for Nancy will take place. A few days later Henry attended Nancy's funeral and then made his way back to the hospital. The doctor was waiting for him.

" Henry if Kaccha's condition remains stable for another week without any problems, she will be ready to go home or go to the long-term facility that I talked to you about."

" I have to get back to work on Monday is there a way you can postpone your decision for another month?"

" I wish I could, but hospital rules are if a patient can be moved or discharged, we cannot prolong their stay at the hospital. Here is the number of a company that rents, sells medical equipment and all the medical supplies you will need."

The doctor provided Henry with a list of equipment and products that he will need, he also mentioned, the company also provides medical assistance at home.

Henry called the company for information, when he hung up the phone, he was dishearten with all the expenses involved in preparing his house and taking care of Kaccha at home. He was thinking, long term care in a facility is also very expensive and he would have to move and find a new job close by so that he would be able to visit Kaccha every day.

" Henry, have you come to a decision?"

" Yes, doctor I have made a decision, I will bring Kaccha home, long term care is costly I would have to move, beside I can't look for a new job I need to pay back the school board, so I will get the house ready for Kaccha for her to come home."

" You better start making preparations soon because I estimate maybe another week here at the most before Kaccha goes home."

Henry contacted human resources where Kaccha worked and human's resources at his workplace to find out what the insurance covered or did not cover with the long-term medical expenditures. Henry was not impressed with the type of coverage Kaccha was entitled to. Henry's insurance would not cover anything because Kaccha had her own insurance.

It was up to Kaccha's insurance to defray the cost for Kaccha's care. Her insurance will only cover fifty percent of the cost for the equipment and short-term coverage of only three months for having a nurse at home to look after Kaccha. The one good thing in all of this is her insurance will cover eighty percent of the cost of the medication needed.

The doctor approached Henry.

" Henry Kaccha will be going home in four days."

" My, my it does not leave me a whole lot of time to be ready, I have to move my ass to make sure everything she will need is in place. Thank you doctor for the heads up."

" Henry went back to work, after work he contacted the company to get the wheels in motion. It would be cheaper to buy the equipment needed than renting. They assured Henry, when Kaccha would be coming home, the house would be ready to accommodate her return home.

When everything was said and done the invoice for the equipment would total sixteen thousand dollars.

Henry was relieved that at least he would be reimbursed for half of the setup cost. The fee for the nurse was also extravagant one thousand dollars a week. Henry was trying to think of a way to keep the nurse after three months the salary for the nurse will come from his pockets.

Henry was walking on pins and needles to get the house ready and Kaccha returning home. At the end of the day, Henry would go to the hospital to spend the night with Kaccha. The day before Kaccha was supposed to be released from the hospital, the doctor approached Henry.

" Henry how are you doing my friend?"

" Nervous as hell."

" I can very well understand, Kaccha will not be going home tomorrow, it looks like Kaccha might be coming down with something, I want to keep her here for at least another week, just to make sure. You know Henry in her condition she is vulnerable for infections and viruses."

" Yes, I know, another week that's fine by me."

CHAPTER 9

Everything was set, after a ten-day delay Kaccha was ready to go home. Henry was happy Kaccha will be finally home. Final preparations were finalized at the hospital.

Kaccha would go home the following morning. The next morning Kaccha was finally going home, as a precaution the nurse that will be taking care of Kaccha tagged along.

Henry was excited and happy, Kaccha was coming home. His excitement did not last long. He was not aware there would be a fee of five hundred dollars to bring Kaccha home.

He assumed it would be free of charge, but he was wrong, Henry was not made aware there would be a cost for moving Kaccha from the hospital to their home. Imagine his surprise when the ambulance driver handed him an invoice.

" What's this?"

" An invoice sir."

" A what?"

" An invoice for the transfer of your wife from the hospital to your home sir."

" There was never any mention of an invoice, the transfer of a patient is supposed to be free."

" Yes, sir they are but only when a hospital patient needs to be transferred to another hospital, there is no cost. In your case sir it was a transfer from the hospital to your home, there is a cost of five hundred dollars for the service. You have ten days to pay."

" That's ridiculous five hundred dollars, you guys are like leeches."

" I am sorry you feel that way sir, the fee has nothing to do with me I am only the driver so please do not shoot the messenger. You can always file a complaint, but I agree with you sir, you should have been told there would be a fee. We have to go, good luck."

Henry was fuming, he would not bother to put in a complaint, it would fall on deaf ears anyway. The fee will put a dent in his budget, he was thrown a curve ball. He said to himself.

" I will need to check my bank account."

The nurse that would be taking care of Kaccha approached Henry.

" Quite the surprise sir."

" Indeed, it's like receiving a sucker punch, you never seen it coming. "

" Ok sir I need you to sign here. It's the agreement that you negotiated with the company for taking care of your wife. My name is Nicole, I am a registered nurse, I will be here Sir Monday to Friday eight am to five pm. All the information you need sir is in this envelope, if for some reason sir, I cannot come in to work, the company will send a replacement."

Nicole hands over the envelope to Henry and walks to the corner of the room to finish putting everything in its place for easy access.

" You have the same name of one of my stepsisters. Are you married Nicole, any kids.? If you think that I am to forward with my questions let me know? I am only trying to get to know you a little better, you will be here five days a week. It would be awkward for the both of us to remain strangers."

" No sir it's quite alright, I am married with three girls, aged twelve, ten and seven. Believe me sir they are a handful; they keep me on my toes."

" I bet they do, three girls, it won't be long before you're going to have to chase the boys away. I have a brother in the army. He was promoted to sergeant, and he is in Afghanistan, my two sisters live in Green Bay. They both work for Macy's, and they share a apartment. "

" I think that my oldest Stephanie, has a humongous crush on a boy in her class named steven. She talks about him all the time, so the raging hormones have been activated. My husband Richard came up with a very good line that goes like this. If a young man comes knocking at our door and asks for Stephanie. He will say, you can come in young man but every three boys that comes knocking at the door, I shoot one and the second boy just left through the back door. It remains to be seen if he will scare them with his famous phrase."

" I have to admit it's a good one, if I was one of the boys who received the warning, I would think twice before coming back. What does your husband do for a living?"

" He works for a trucking firm; he is in charge of the shipping and receiving department."

" I am a grade ten math teacher. Poor Kaccha worked for a chemical company. Nicole here is my daily schedule. I leave for work at eight o'clock in the morning, I get home between four fifteen and four thirty, depends on the traffic and one more thing don't call me sir, my name is Henry. All the information about her condition and daily medicine is in the red binder on the table. "

" Ok good, can I bring it home with me tonight so that I can educate myself with the content in the binder?"

" Certainly, and fyi there is another copy of the binder on top of the fridge. "

" Talking about the fridge sir is it ok that I put my lunch in the fridge and use the microwave to warm it up? "

" Of course, no need to ask, I want you to feel right at home, while your here my house is your house and here is a set of keys for the house in case you ever need them."

" Thank you sir, sorry I mean Sir Henry, I will see you in the morning. "

" Well, well, what do we have here a comedian?"

" Maybe, good night, Henry. My phone number is on a sticky note on the fridge."

" That reminds me, I should also give you my number, here is my number good night, Nicole."

" If you need my help, do not hesitate to call me. "

Henry set up a cot only a few feet away from Kaccha's bed. He then sat at the kitchen table to try to put a budget together, it took him all evening to come up with a good budget. Henry was exhausted. He took a quick peek at Kaccha to make sure everything was fine, set his alarm clock, laid down on the cot in a matter of minutes Henry was in snooze Ville.

A beeping sound woke up Henry, a timer connected to one of the tubes connected to Kaccha was beeping, Henry had no clue what to do, so he called Nicole.

" Hello. "

" Nicole. "

" I apologize for calling you in the middle of the night, the timer connected to a tube is beeping. "

" No need to worry Henry, I know which one you are talking about before going to bed, did you reset the timer?"

" No, I was not aware that I was supposed to reset a timer. "

" My apologies Henry it completely slipped my mind to tell you. Look on the small table beside her bed, there is a sheet of paper with instructions of things that needs to be done before going to bed. "

" Ok I have the paper in my hands, I need to reset the timer to zero, from what I can see, there is only one timer. What a relief only one timer. With all the gadgets hooked up to Kaccha I'm trying to remember which is which. "

" That's correct Henry only one timer, reset the timer to zero and your troubles for tonight will be over. "

" May I ask what the timer is for?"

" It is a timer to let us know it is time to feed Kaccha. It is a precautionary measure in case we forget to feed Kaccha."

" Thanks a million, Nicole see you in the morning."

The following day Henry called his mother to give her the news that Kaccha was finally home. She was happy for Henry that Kaccha was home. They also talked about Mr. Moore's health. She was very worried about Mr. Moore's health issues, especially is heart, and no news from Lucas for the past two weeks.

" Everyday nurse Nicole would take notes of the day's events when Henry would come home from work, is first priority was reading the notes and putting the notes away when done in a filing cabinet. One day at work, Henry noticed a donation jar with his name on it.

" Janice what's this?"

" We decided to put a donation jar on the counter to help you with your financial burden and every two weeks there will be a fifty/fifty draw with the proceeds going to you."

" Who is in charge for the draw?"

" Me Henry, it's the least we can do to help you, you're going through very difficult times, and we want to help."

" Thank you so very, very, very much you do not know what this means to me, I am at a loss for words. What can I do to show you, my gratitude?"

" No need for you to do something to show your gratitude. We are not only friends when everything is fine, we are also your friends when you need help."

" You guys are the best coworkers a guy can have. I am blessed to work with such great caring people."

The money from the donation can and the fifty/fifty draw Henry put the money away in a box for safe keeping. One night Henry got a call from his mom, his dad passed away.

" Henry I am so sorry to tell you this, your dad passed away a few hours ago. His health started deteriorating twenty-four hours ago, he was rushed to the hospital where he suffered a massive heart attack."

" No, no, no, no, mom it's the middle of the night you're dreaming mom, wake up mom this is only a dream."

" I wish it was."

" Have you contacted Lucas, Nicole, and Julie yet?"

" Yes, the girls will be here tomorrow. It will take Lucas three days to arrive. Henry I am devastated, I don't know what I am going to do without him. Married for thirty-seven years and a three-year courtship before we married, all in all forty years by his side. "

" Mom I will make arrangements tomorrow for the care of Kaccha for a couple of days, and the day after tomorrow, I will fly out to Chicago. Hang in their mom, we will all be there soon. Love you mom."

" Love you too, see you soon. "

Henry was in tears, he could not believe Mr. Morris was gone, he was a rock for him, you always see your parents as invincible, in the morning he contacted his boss to let him know that his dad passed away and he would be absent for a week. The next morning Henry talked to nurse Nicole if she could stay at his house until he returns home.

" Of course, I will stay Henry and do not worry everything will be under control. I am so sorry for your lost. "

The next morning, he was on a plane on route to Chicago. His mom was waiting for him at the airport. His two sisters were already at the house. Not much was said on the way home. The next day Lucas and Sandra finally arrived. They embraced, everyone was crying, their mom was trying to stay strong and composed but it was not easy.

Lucas introduced Sandra to Nicole and Julie. "

Sandra replied.

" I am happy to finally meet you, I wish it was for different circumstances. "

" Lucas, the funeral is in two days."

" Mom sit down, did you hear the sound of your voice, you should go take a nap."

" I cannot sleep without your father by my side. Only sixty-one years old and already gone."

" You should go see a doctor; he will give you something to help you sleep. I will go with you tomorrow to see a doctor."

" Thanks for the offer, Lucas, I don't think it is necessary, I do not want to start taking sleeping pills, they are addictive. "

" It would be only for a few weeks mom. "

" I said no, no is no."

The funeral was held at the local cemetery. A small gathering of relatives and friends. When the priest said is final words, Mrs. Moore lost consciousness, she could not bear the fact that her husband will be six feet in the ground and decomposing.

When she regained consciousness, Lucas and his sisters helped their mom to get to the car. Once home Mrs. Moore opened the floodgates with uncontrollable crying.

" I am so sorry for losing control, I can't help it, I am overwhelmed right now. "

" Mom, you need to sit down before you fall again. Here mom I brought you a chair.

" Thanks Henry."

" I will never be able to sit in the blue chair next to the sofa, it was his favorite chair when watching television, all his stuff is still here, as if he was only gone doing errands and come back home in time for lunch. "

Nicole was curious to know when everybody was leaving

" Lucas when do you have to go back?"

" We have to leave the day after tomorrow."

" Lucas, mom told me you were promoted to sergeant, congrats. "

" Thank you and you Henry when are you going back home?"

" Tomorrow. I would love to stay a little longer, but Kaccha needs me."

" It's ok we understand any changes in her condition?"

" Unfortunately, no."

" Lucas how is it going for you in Afghanistan?"

" We patrol ahead of a convoy to try to prevent an ambush that could easily destroy the convoy. "

" No fire fights so far."

" No mom we do get sporadic contact with the enemy, nothing serious, when I get back from a patrol Sandra always greets me with a grin from ear-to-ear right honey?"

" Yes indeed, I am always happy to see everyone coming back to basecamp. For the moment I am assigned to the first aid station. "

" That's good it keeps you from arm's way. "

Yes, it does, and I cannot wait for Lucas to come back from a patrol. "

" And you guys my dear sisters when are you leaving?"

" We need to get going tomorrow after lunch."

" Here we are the family together, starting tomorrow you will all go your separate ways. I wish I had the power to keep you all here with me."

Henry called Nicole to let her know that he would be home tomorrow evening.

Everybody was trying their best to keep their mom calm. At the end of the evening, she was more composed, she was able to have conversations without any tears. The family was aware that it would be an uphill battle for their mother to cope without their dad. The next day Henry was on his way home. He was anxious to come back home and be with Kaccha. When he arrived home his first questions where.

" Hi Nicole so anything new, situation still the same?"

" Yes, still the same and you Henry how are you feeling, are you ok?"

" Yes, I am fine thank you for asking, it always takes time to comprehend the passing of a loved one, life will never be the same. You know there is a saying that goes like this, time heals everything time does not heal everything it helps you cope. After all these years, I still hurt for the loss of my parents because of a car crash when I was only eight years old. "

" That is so true, are you alright for the remainder of the evening, I can stay a little longer if you like?"

" No, you can go home, did you write down all the extra hours for staying here?"

" Already done sir, in the notepad on the kitchen table, well good night, talk to you in the morning."

Henry paid Nicole for her extra hours of work. The three months free service was coming to an end soon, Henry will have to make financial adjustments. When he purchased the equipment that was needed, he sold the car that Kaccha owned. Thank goodness it was all paid for. He saved the money he received from Kaccha's insurance; Henry had to pay all expenses upfront before being reimbursed fifty percent of the cost.

Henry took the money out of the box, money raised by friends at work, to calculate the amount of money that was in the box. One thousand seven hundred, fifty-two dollars. Not too shabby for a donation box and fifty/fifty draws, money in the bank, eleven thousand dollars, including the money reimbursed from Kaccha's insurance company.

The money will keep him afloat for at least two months. Henry was busting his brain to find a way to get more money in his bank account. The only solution was selling his car. Which meant Henry would commute back and forth to work by bus.

Henry fell asleep at the kitchen table. When Nicole was unlocking the door, Henry was awakened by the noise. When Nicole entered the house, Henry was standing in the kitchen still half asleep.

" Henry are you alright? No offense but you look like a zombie this morning."

" None taken, I am a little stiff this morning, I fell asleep at the kitchen table, the chair and the table are not quite as comfortable as my cot. "

" Are you going to work this morning?"

" Yes, no shower and shave for me this morning, a quick change of clothes and I am out of here."

It took Henry five minutes to get ready. He did not want to be late. Once at work he noticed the donation jar was no longer on the shelf and at the end of the week no fifty/fifty draw. Janice approached Henry and said.

" No one was putting money in the jar anymore and with my new responsibilities I could no longer find the time to sell tickets. "

Henry understood and thanked her for everything she did for him one. night Henry was standing at the foot of the bed Kaccha was looking in his direction. Henry could not wait to tell Nicole the good news, Kaccha was looking at him. The next morning as soon as Nicole came in the door. Henry ran to her and said.

" Nicole Kaccha looked at me last night her eyes were looking at me. That means that she is starting to remember who I am."

" Sorry to burst your bubble Henry, her eyes might have stopped on you, that does not mean she is able to recognize you, she may open her eyes, wake up and fall asleep at regular intervals, and have basic reflexes, such as blinking when she is startled by a loud noise or withdrawing her hand when it is squeezed hard. "

" I was so hopeful that it meant she was improving. Every night I pray and ask God if there is something he can do to make Kaccha feel better or if I can switch places with Kaccha, you know Kaccha healthy and me bedridden, I never get an answer. Every morning I recite her a poem that I wrote the night before. I love her more and more each day, it's hard to see her like this and accept the fact there is no coming back for her, she deserves a better fate than this. Well, I better go I am going to be late, have a good day."

Nicole watched Henry leaving for work she was thinking what a sweet caring man. His love and devotion for Kaccha is unbelievable, you have to see it to believe it. This was you call true love.

She was under the assumption true love only existed in movies and fairy tales. Henry is a rare breed, most men by now would have given up and placed her in a long-term medical facility, find a new girlfriend, but not Henry he is sticking to his guns to keep his promise. It makes me sad. This couple did not deserve to be in this predicament.

Henry received a letter in the mail to advise him, the price of the medication that Kaccha needs everyday will be going up by five percent. It was costing Henry over one hundred dollars a week to cover the cost of the twenty percent of her medication he needed to pay.

The ultimate test of survival was close at hand, only one more week before the three months that covers Nicole's salary will expire. After that he will be on his own. Henry started doing online surveys to make extra money. Henry sold his car.

The money from the sale of his car and the money that Henry put aside will come in handy to be able to pay Nicole for sixteen weeks. One night there was a knock at his door, it was his friend James

" What a pleasant surprise please come in."

" Thanks, how are things with you?"

" No changes in Kaccha, I am about to run out of money to keep Kaccha here, I might not have a choice but to move her to the long-term facility which is over an hour and a half away if I want to keep on working. Yes, the facility is expensive but at least I will be able to keep my job, and you James how are things going for you?"

" I am getting used of living alone. It was tough going for the first couple of weeks coming home to an empty house. Henry you might think that I am crazy but every time I come home, I can see her for a few seconds wearing her favorite dress, sitting at the kitchen table looking at me and smiling?

" Well James that means she wants to let you know; she is in heaven waiting for you."

" James was looking at Kaccha,

" Such a shame, a happy beautiful woman married to a good man with many years of happiness in front of her."

" You know James I feel guilty."

" Why do you feel guilty?"

" Well, if I had not gone to South Africa to go look for my sister, she knew I was going to call, she was probably running late and stumbled down the stairs, that or God punished her for deceiving her parents for coming to the "U. S" to be with me."

" Come on Henry do you actually believe you're the one responsible for her accident? Do you remember what you told me in the hospital hallway the day my wife died? "

" Yes, I do remember but I cannot get that guilty feeling out of my head. "

" You should follow your own advice. I hope for your sake, one day you will realize you had nothing to do with her mishap, come on now you know it does not make any sense."

" Anyway, James I am really happy for you that you were able to find a way to cope everyday life without your wife. "

" Henry I am here tonight because I wanted to know how you were doing and to bring you this box, go ahead open it."

" What's this?"

" I knew that you would be needing money to keep Kaccha at home, so I held a fundraiser in your honor my dear friend, it's the least I could do for you. "

" Thanks James you're a true friend, I owe you one my friend."

" You owe me nothing, now count the money."

" Wow four thousand and eighty dollars."

" Yes, did I mention, I love bowling so last Saturday myself and my bowling buddies, raised the funds with a bowling tournament."

" Thanks again James, I will never forget this, and don't forget to say thank you to everyone for their big generosity, you can assure them, the money will be put to good use."

" They know the fundraiser was for a good cause and the much-needed money will help you to keep Kaccha at home."

When James was leaving, Henry hugged him, thanked him again and again for taking that extra step to help him. Henry set aside the money in his box and went to bed. A few months later Henry sold most of his furniture, cancelled the home phone and cable service.

The only furniture remaining in the house was his cot, a small table in the kitchen, fridge, stove, washer and dryer, microwave, a couch in the living room and a small desk, a chair, and his computer.

The only remaining service in the house was electricity, his cell phone service and internet which he needed for work. Henry was distressed and came to a painful decision if he was to keep his job Kaccha would need to be moved to the long-term care facility.

He could not see or think of another option. He contacted the facility. Kaccha will be moved at the beginning of the following month, which meant, the move would take place in ten days. Henry broke the news to Nicole, that Kaccha would be moving to the long-term facility in ten days. Nicole was saddened by the news but understood it was best for both Kaccha and Henry.

Henry let her know it was not because of her service. He praised her on her work, moving Kaccha was the only solution that he could think of. He called his mom to let her know about Kaccha being moved to the long-term care facility.

" Hi mom how are you today? I am calling to let you know that in a week Kaccha will be moved to a long care facility."

" I am managing thank you for asking and moving Kaccha it's for the best."

" I know but I do not like it, I am breaking my promise."

" Henry you are not breaking any promise, you did what you could, you're not abandoning her. It's a win win situation for the both of you."

" I guess your right thanks mom talk to you later bye bye."

" Bye Henry."

The following morning Henry had this to say to Nicole.

" My heart is in million pieces right now, I tried my best, I exhausted all possible alternatives to keep Kaccha at home and you Nicole will you be out of a job. "

" No there is a waiting list for people needing help at home, when I am done here, I will have another client to take care of. One question Henry have you notified my employer?"

" Shoot no, I knew there was something else I needed to do."

" No worries, Henry, I will take care of that for you. You know I try not to get too close to the patients, but it is easier said than done."

" Same here you are not just a nurse taking care of my wife. I have come to think of you as a friend."

" Me too Henry after all we are only human."

" We'll have a good day Nicole; I will see you later."

" Thank you, Henry, have a good day at work."

The dreaded day to move Kaccha was only twenty-four hours away. Henry could not sleep, filled with regrets and guilt, he was letting Kaccha down. The next morning Nicole and the special unit truck arrived and took Kaccha away. Henry took the day off to accompany Kaccha to her new residence.

Henry borrowed James's car, following the truck, Henry was trying very hard to control is emotions. When Kaccha was admitted to her room, Henry was relieved. It was a very clean building, a friendly staff, at the end of the day Nicole said her tearful goodbye to Henry and wished him all the best. Henry kissed Kaccha goodnight and was on his way home.

Henry would come home to an empty house but not for long.

CHAPTER 10

While all the changes that were taking place back home. Lucas was having his own problems in Afghanistan. His platoon was to scout and patrol a road that led to a small village, set up defensive positions on both sides of the road ahead of a humanitarian convoy carrying food and medication to the residents of the small village.

Before leaving that faithful morning, Lucas was briefed one last time with the details on the task at hand. He was also advised to be very careful, because the latest reports showed heavy enemy presence and movement in the area,

" So be very diligent and be on the lookout for snipers and be very careful not to walk into a ambush. "

" Yes sir."

" You are very well aware that last week two platoons were ambushed with heavy casualties. Oh yes your girlfriend Sandra will be one of the medics today."

" Yes sir."

" Dismissed and good luck."

Two interpreters will accompany the platoon. Lucas would be leading a thirty-two-man platoon which included two medics. On missions

Lucas treated Sandra no different from the other soldiers in the platoon. Putting his feelings aside and get the job done.

Lucas again briefed his men on the mission and to get ready to move in one hour. The convoy would be leaving in five hours. Seven am the platoon started moving, not knowing, one of the interpreters was a spy for the enemy. Lucas and his men were heading straight for a well-organized camouflaged ambush of over one hundred enemy fighters.

Before leaving the sergeant that was ambushed the previous week pinpointed to Lucas the areas to avoid.

" Seems to me captain we will have a lot of zigzagging to do that will slow us down. The convoy might end up in front of us."

" I know Lucas, but it is the only way to go. "

" Ok sir anything else?"

" Captain O'Brien who will be leading the convoy is aware of the delays it might bring. That is why the convoy will be leaving the base five hours behind you. It's fifteen miles stretch of road with mountains on both sides of the road. Ideal terrain for the enemy to set an ambush. Good luck and be careful, bring back your men safe and sound."

The comment of bring his men back safe and sound was wearing heavy on Lucas's mind. He was responsible for their safety, his men trusted him. He knew they would follow him anywhere, that's how confident they were, and they knew he would not send them somewhere that he would not go himself

The platoon slowly made their way along the side of the road. As instructed by his commanding officer, Lucas was taking detours along the way to keep his platoon from being ambushed.

When they reached the halfway point of their destination, one of the interpreters started running and all hell broke loose. They were hit with mortars, heavy machine gunfire. The platoon was out in the open.

Before Lucas was able to organize a defense parameter, half of his men were either dead or wounded. Sandra and the other medic were killed.

To make things worse, the interpreter that ran was able to get away. Bullets, mortars, rpg's were coming from all directions. Lucas called for immediate air support and evac for the wounded. Both where denied, no air support available because it was on standby to protect the convoy and no evac because of the volume of fire they were receiving.

They were able to retreat in a ditch on the side of the road. Lucas waved for his men to hold their fire, to fix bayonets, to put their grenades on the ground in front of them and reload with fresh magazines and not to move an inch. Lucas signaled to his men when he gives the signal the men were to throw one grenade and start shooting, a few men were assigned to throw smoke grenades.

The purpose for his men to hold their fire was to make the enemy think they were all dead, the enemy would come out of their hiding place to retrieve the weapons of the dead soldiers and kill the wounded. The wounded were yelling for help. Lucas was feeling a sense of guilt for leaving the wounded behind.

" His plan worked, after ten minutes, the fighters slowly came out of their hiding places. There was a premature celebration thinking that all the Americans were dead.

When they were close enough, Lucas gave the signal, the enemy was caught in the open, they were dropping like flies. Lucas gave the signal to pop some smoke, they retrieved some of the wounded and retreated to find a place to hide for the night.

Lucas received word, the convoy was attacked and nearly destroyed with heavy casualties, one of the casualties was captain O'Brien a twenty-two-year veteran. Out of ten trucks only two trucks and a handful of survivors made it back to the basecamp. One Apache helicopter was shot down, another Apache helicopter was badly damaged but was able to make it to base.

Lucas ordered his men to form a defensive parameter around a small house. Fourteen of his men were either killed or wounded. He ordered a few of his men to go retrieve the wounded, they were killed by enemy fire. He had no choice but to leave some of the wounded behind. They were only able to retrieve two of the wounded.

Lucas contacted the base for immediate extraction. Negative they would have to wait until morning. They were down two helicopters and taking care of the remnants from the convoy.

It was pouring rain, Lucas made sure none of his men took refuge in the house. At daybreak the small house was shattered by a RPG, they could see a large group of enemy soldiers coming down the hill about four hundred feet from their defensive positions.

Lucas knew they were in for the fight of their lives. His only hope was that air support could reach them in time so they could make a hasty retreat and evacuate back to base. The depleted platoon came under heavy fire. A few minutes before help arrived, a mortar round took out his radioman and slightly wounding Lucas.

When the Apache helicopters arrived and pounding the enemy soldiers, Lucas and a handful of his men were able to make it to waiting helicopters to evacuate and bring them back to base. Lucas was aware that Sandra was one of the casualties that was left behind.

When the helicopters landed at the main basecamp, only seven of his men including three wounded stepped out of the helicopter. Out of thirty-three men including himself. The interpreter was dead Lucas was devastated knowing that Sandra was left in the kill zone. Only seven of his men with two critically wounded and one slightly wounded.

One of the wounded soldiers died on the operating table. Bringing down the total to six of his men to have survived the battle. Lucas was shell shocked and would never be the same again. When Lucas stepped out of the helicopter, his commanding officer was there to meet him, Lucas was speechless, Lucas looked at him with a look of despair in his eyes.

He silently walked to the first aid station without saying a word. A medic tried talking to him, but he was not listening. All he could think of was his men and especially Sandra that were left behind on the battlefield.

He blamed himself for leading his platoon in an ambush. After receiving help to clean the small wound on his right leg. The medic tried her best to communicate with him. He did not want to talk to anyone because he was getting ready to go retrieve his men left behind on the battlefield. His commanding officer stepped in the first aid station saw Lucas getting ready to go out again.

" Where do you think you are going sergeant?"

" I am going to retrieve my men from the battlefield sir."

" Can you tell me sergeant who gave you the order to go out there?"

" No one sir, I am going on my own."

" Sergeant listen to me you will not come back alive and if you do you are looking at a court martial for insubordination and the chance of being dismissed from the army. "

" Sir I gave my word to the men, sir that I will leave no one behind"

" Well sergeant from what I hear from your men sir. They are still here because of you. Yes, I know sergeant some of your men did not come back, but it's war. You cannot predict the outcome when you're in a firefight. Some of your men came back because of you. You displayed good leadership sergeant, the men said they would follow you anywhere."

" What about the men we left behind sir."

" A convoy of three trucks and fifty men are on their way to bring them back here. From what I heard you were valiant and always the last one to retreat. Apparently, you did a lot of damage to an enemy company. They are now in a non-combatant role until they get more men to replace the ones your platoon killed. Against overwhelming odds, you were able to keep the enemy at bay and bring back some of your men."

" But Sandra sir. "

" They will retrieve every man in your company and bring them back."

" Ok sir I will stay put. "

" Wise decision sergeant, report to my tent in one hour for a debriefing understood."

" Yes, sir one hour a debriefing in your tent."

" See you then sergeant."

When the trucks arrived with the dead soldiers Lucas grabbed Sandra's lifeless body he was crying and apologizing to his men that were killed. His commanding officer approached him.

" Come with me please you do not need to see this. You know you did your best."

" No leave me alone, I need to attend to my men and especially Sandra, she needs me and no debriefing for me today or ever. "

Lucas could not function as a soldier anymore, even with a lot of help, he was not able to come out of the bubble he was in. Sandra was dead because of him, he received a honorary discharge from the army and shipped back to the states.

His problem was, in his head, he was reliving the battle over and over, hearing his wounded men crying for help. With no other choice he had to leave them behind. His biggest problem was he knew the wounded left behind would be butchered by the enemy. The guilt trip will not go away, he lost the love of his life.

Mrs. Moore called Henry to give him the news that Lucas was discharged from the army due to health issues and Sandra was killed in action. Henry's emotions got the best of him and started crying. He could not believe what he was hearing, Lucas's sick, Sandra killed.

Lucas was not the same person he was before the ambush and having to leave his men and Sandra behind. He is tormented with guilt. Lucas was coming home to live with her. She also advised Henry; her house was for sale. Henry was devastated by the news about Lucas.

Henry was also feeling guilty about Kaccha not being home where she belonged, after a month, Kaccha was brought back home. Henry knew with Kaccha back home, it will financially ruin him. But he wanted to keep his promise to Kaccha.

Friends from work tried to make him understand with Kaccha at the long care facility he was not abandoning her. It was the best scenario for both himself and Kaccha, she was at the right place and Henry could keep on working. Nothing could convince him to let Kaccha stay at the facility, he was bringing her back home where she belonged.

When he called his mother about his decision to bring Kaccha home, she was angry, frustrated with Henry bringing Kaccha home

" Henry by bringing Kaccha back home, your committing financial suicide do you know that?"

" Not really mom, I can keep working and pay a nurse to take care of Kaccha when I am at work."

" For how long will you be able to pay the nurse?"

" I do not know mom it all depends. "

" Depends on what Henry?"

" I am looking at other options."

" Listen Henry, I know you made her a promise, but sometimes there is no choice but to break a promise. Don't you think she is receiving better care at the long-term facility?"

" Yes and no, yes, she would receive better care, but she is alone for five days a week. I cannot leave her alone. I tried it for a month, I was unable to accept the fact that she was not home and alone with strangers."

" Come on Henry use your common sense with you taking a very bad decision and Lucas mentally wounded from the war, I do not know what direction to take anymore."

" Have faith in me mom I will find a solution."

" I cannot believe that you are that stupid to think you will find a solution, there is no other solution than Kaccha staying put at the long care facility."

" Mom, I do not like the fact that you are calling me stupid."

" You are stupid for the way you think, and do not call me mom anymore, I am not your biological mother, I liked you Henry but never considered you as my son. You have my blood boiling. If someone would take my temperature right now, they would say I was ready to explode."

" Come on please do not talk like that."

" Well, what do you want me to say? I have to go now."

She ended the conversation without even saying goodbye. He was sad about the conversation with his mother. Another spike in my coffin. I was never her son, she liked me but did not love me. There goes another piece of my heart.

I hope when she calms down, she will call me back. She never did call back. Henry was really hurting, not knowing the whereabouts of his sister, Mr. Moore passed away. The war took its toll on Lucas. His mentor, his best friend was suffering with mental issues.

Henry called the company if nurse Nicole was available, he was told she was not available, she was busy with another stay-at-home client. Henry was in a bind. He was able to find a replacement for Nicole, after only five weeks he let her go.

Henry exhausted every possible avenue to stay afloat. Henry could no longer find funds to pay for the nurse. Henry tried to cash in his retirement pension from the school board. The money from the pension plan could not be withdrawn until he was sixty years old.

Henry had no choice but to quit his job and try to find some work online so that he could work from home. Henry was successful to find work with an advertising company. He was earning peanuts compared to his job as a teacher.

At the end of the day, he would surf the internet to find a better paying job. To make things worse. Henry received a registered letter from the school board to inform him by leaving his job he did not honor his agreement to work a year with only two thirds of his salary. He needed to cough up seven thousand dollars, within thirty days upon receipt of the letter, or face having to go in front of a judge.

 A few weeks after receiving the threatening letter, Henry received a phone call from Mrs. Moore to let him know, the house was sold. Henry was hopeful she was calling to give him a portion of the profit she made by selling the house. When he answered the phone. He told Mrs. Moore with an upbeat tone of voice he was happy she was calling.

" Hi mom how are you?" I hope you are calling me so we can be bygones be bygones."

" Did I not tell you not to call me mom anymore? So anyway, I want you to know, the house is sold. By now you must be scratching your head every day to think of something to resolve your issue of having no more money."

" Hi, I am sorry Mrs. Moore, I hope that you do not feel obligated."

She cut him off

" What do you mean obligated? I am not calling to give you money. You will not get a single penny from me. You know why Henry? "

" Sorry Mrs. Moore, I assumed."

Again, she cut him off.

" Ok I get it, you assumed I was contacting you to give you some of my money. You know I do not approve of your situation with Kaccha being home, so why waste my money for something I do not agree with. I called to let you know, we are moving and that I disown you. With Steve gone, I no longer have to pretend that I love you. So good luck and goodbye."

" Wait can I at least talk to Lucas please?"

" Lucas is sleeping."

" Can I ask you one final question. Did I do or say something to personally offend you?"

" Are you serious? You are more stupid than I thought, goodbye Henry."

Poor Henry was crying when he hung up the phone and trying to decipher what Mrs. Morris said. He could not come up with an answer.

" I know in my heart I am doing the right thing having Kaccha here with me, I will never, never, never abandon her, turn my back on her. She is my wife. The only woman who captured my heart and let me capture her heart. We were enjoying such a wonderful life together."

Henry was also filled with remorse because he was away looking for his sister. He kept on thinking if I would have stayed home instead of going on a quest to find my sister. She would not have rushed going down the stairs to get home, to not miss my phone call.

I can still see her smiling face sending me kisses, her hands shaped like a heart. When I boarded the place, I took a quick glance, she was still standing in the same spot waving me goodbye. I will always treasure that moment. Maybe I am a fool, but I cannot spend one more day with Kacca not being home. She is still the love of my life and always will be. His phone rang.

" Hello."

" Henry it's Lucas."

" I am so happy to hear your voice."

" Henry you must know by now, that I am no longer in the army and Sandra was killed in action because of me. I have a very hard time to function on a daily basis. I am home but the men from my platoon did not get the chance to go home to their families. I led them into a ambush, the enemy soldiers cut us to pieces before we had a chance to react. I should have been able to see the signs of an ambush."

" Listen Lucas you must have heard the same thing now a thousand times, you did your best under extreme circumstances. You know that some of your men were able to go home because of you."

" I know but if I would have done better, more of my men and Sandra would be going home. I was foolish to accept the promotion to sergeant."

" Talking about foolish your mom says I am stupid for keeping Kaccha at home, she might be right, but I cannot change the way I feel."

" Why did you say your mom instead of mom?"

" Well, she said she liked me, but never loved me and she disowned me, she does not have to pretend anymore."

" Wow I was not aware she felt that way about you, it's a shame. I could she not love you? Anyway, I do know how you feel because I cannot change the feeling of guilt and remorse for the men under my command who perished on the battlefield. It is driving me bananas, I talk to a shrink every week it helps me cope, I am not the same man, you used to know, sometimes when I am alone, I get dark ideas. You know put an end to all this. "

" Please don't do that, I do not want to lose my big brother. You are all that I have in this world. What about Sandra's parents? "

" I have tried calling but they do not answer the phone or return my messages. I have to go Henry, talk to you soon."

That was the last time Henry would talk to Lucas. Henry tried to call Lucas several times on his cellphone when someone finally answered the phone, he was told Lucas tried to commit suicide, he was now in a mental institution. Mrs. Moore never contacted Henry again. He was on his own. Henry's financial burden hit the skids. In a short period of time, he will be penniless.

CHAPTER 11

Henry is caressing Kaccha's face and reciting loving words to her.

" Kaccha my darling I love you more than yesterday but less than tomorrow. You are more beautiful now than the day I met you, my little butterfly, my little flower dancing in the wind. No matter what the financial institutions do to me I will never let go, my precious angel, some say I am crazy, they are right but for the wrong reasons, I am crazy in love with you and always will be."

Henry hears a knock at the door, when Henry opened the door, a man handed him an envelope.

" You have been served, good day sir."

Henry closed the door, opened the envelope, his jaw dropped to the floor, the envelope contained an affidavit to appear in court. The school board wanted their money.

The money Henry was earning with his online job was not even enough to keep him afloat. All of his extra money was gone. It was only a question of time before the bank will repossess the house for non-payment. When Henry appeared in court, he was successful to postpone the hearing for a later date.

With all the stress and anxiety Henry's health was going downhill. He vowed to stay strong and not let his health get in the way. He had no choice but to declare bankruptcy. The bank advised him he needed to be out of the house in thirty days. He decided to call his friend James if he could help him find a place to live.

" James it's Henry."

" Henry."

" Yes, it's me how are things going for you?"

" Ok I guess."

" James, I have to move out of the house in thirty days, I declared bankruptcy, I was wondering if you knew where I could find a place that is not too expensive."

" You can always move here buddy."

" Thanks for the generous offer my friend but no, I would not want to be a burden."

" I understand I would probably feel the same way, we are always afraid to be a burden for someone. I might know of a place that is for rent. Let me make a few phone calls and I will call you back. "

Within an hour James called back to inform Henry, the place was still for rent.

" I put in a good word for you and explained your situation, so he is willing to rent it to you for only four hundred dollars a month."

" Thanks a million, my dear friend, there is one thing that came out positive when our wives were in the hospital. We became friends and good friends at that."

" Yes, that's true, I will help you move, but how are you going to move Kaccha?"

" I have no choice I will hire the same moving company, that moved Kaccha here for me, I have to admit they do provide good service and take the time needed to move a patient."

Moving Kaccha depleted the remainder of his bank account. The. Twenty percent cost for Kaccha's, medicine, rent and groceries it will be very hard for Henry to make ends meet. He swallowed his pride and started going to a food bank.

His next court date was approaching, he was worried on what will be decided by the judge. The day that Henry will go to court, his friend James will take care of Kaccha while he is gone.

Henry was a nervous wreck when he again appeared in court. Again, without a lawyer. He was elated when the judge dismissed the case. The judge addressed the lawyer for the school board by saying.

" Mr. Engelbrecht declared bankruptcy for good reasons and how do you expect him to be able to pay the amount of money owed to the school board? "

" Your honor, if Mr. Engelbrecht cannot pay his debt, can you give him a sentence, that he needs to complete the hours remaining to work on the agreement he signed."

" Look at the man does he look healthy enough to go to work."

" But your honor."

" I said the case is dismissed. You seem to be a well-educated man, you should know by now, that you cannot draw blood from a rock."

" Did you take the time to go over the notes for his case?"

" I will ignore that foolish comment, the court is adjourned."

Henry was happy about the verdict, finally something positive for a change. James gave Henry a pat on the shoulder.

" Well done my friend, I am happy for you. One obstacle less to worry about."

" Thanks man, you know James you really are a good friend, most friends will say anytime you need a hand with something don't hesitate to call and when you do call for help. They have all sorts of excuses. Like the saying goes to help a friend in need, is a friend indeed. That's you James. "

" I have always been a man of my word; I am your friend in good times and bad times."

" Yes, you are, guys like you are a rare breed."

" Thanks Henry, anything else for today?"

" No and thanks again."

Henry was happy to at least have someone he could count on when needed. Henry started to cough.

" No, no, no, I cannot be sick, the germs."

Henry tried to call a pharmacy for some advice, but his cell phone service was cancelled for non-payment. Henry drank several glasses of hot water to diminish his cough. Every morning like clockwork, Henry would recite a poem to Kaccha, made sure everything was fine with her, made sure to give her medication, feed her.

He was always careful not to block her feeding tube. He made sure to wash Kaccha every day. Every week he would go to the food bank while James kept an eye on Kaccha. Henry's cough would not go away. He needed to wear a surgical mask when around Kaccha.

" Henry you should go to a clinic, your pale as a ghost, look in the mirror, can you see your bloodshot eyes?"

" I am ok James; I will be fine."

" No, you're not, how will you be able to care of Kaccha, I do not want to be morbid but what if you're sick or worse and if you kick the bucket before her what then? Take my car and go before I boot your ass all the way to the clinic."

" Ok I will go."

James threw his car keys to Henry, and Henry was out the door. A couple hours later, Henry returned from the clinic.

" So, what's the verdict?"

" I have pneumonia. "

" Did he give you a prescription?"

" Yes, take a look at what he prescribed. Good thing I only needed to pay twenty percent of the cost. "

" Be sure to take your medication."

" Yes, dad I will."

They hugged and James was out the door. Henry was extra vigilant when close to Kaccha. He noticed her limbs, muscles were contracted and immovable. He said to himself.

" She is starting to waste away. No god please no."

Everyday poor Henry wished it was him in the bed instead of the delicate beautiful flower he married and love so much. The doctor did advise him, after a period of time her limbs, muscles would become immovable and to be extra careful she might develop recurrent pneumonia.

One morning Henry called 911. Kaccha needed to be hospitalized. The doctor also admitted Henry to the hospital because of his pneumonia. He requested to be in the same room with Kaccha. Permission was denied, he was in the adjacent room. He also requested to have his laptop with him, so that he could work.

After ten days of being bedridden, Henry was released from the hospital, but he remained on the premises to be with Kaccha. A week later Kaccha was ready to go home. The doctor advised Henry to pay close attention for signs of recurring pneumonia because of her immobility and inability to keep secretion out of her lungs. The lungs may collapse overtime.

" If Kaccha is admitted again to the hospital for the same symptoms, she will stay in the hospital, no more going home."

" Ok doctor thank you."

" The ambulance will bring Kaccha home this afternoon."

" Why can she not stay in the hospital?"

" She is well enough to go home, or do you want me to transfer her to the long-term care facility?"

" Will there be a charge to bring her home?"

" No, I will make sure there is no charge to bring her home."

" Thank you very much doctor, I truly appreciate the fact that there will be no fee to bring her home."

" You're welcome and how can we ask you for money when you're broke?"

As planned Kaccha was discharged from the hospital and brought home by ambulance. Henry was no fool, he knew it was the beginning of the end for Kaccha. Henry was a nervous wreck, his concentration was taking a beating, it was getting more and more difficult for him to be able to do his job. He was making too many mistakes.

His boss put him on a one-month probation to see if he could rectify the problem of making mistakes. If is work did not improve after one month, his services with the company would be no longer required.

Henry was working hard to keep his job, his only source of income. Henry needed new clothes, did not have the money to go shopping. James offered him some money, but Henry refused to take the money. It was enough that he relied on the food bank for groceries, he did not want to start relying on James for money. James again offered Henry a place to stay

" Take my offer Henry, I have an empty bedroom."

" Ok if you insist, I will move. I will give my landlord my notice that I am moving."

" Good we are going to be roomies."

" Wait a minute I do not have the money to move Kaccha again."

" I will rent a special vehicle that is rigged, equipped for such a move. You can repay me when you can."

Before moving in with James, Henry sold the remainder of his furniture. Only thing that Henry kept was a few small personal items his laptop and his clothes.

James and Henry prepared the bedroom to accommodate Kaccha. The move was done without any problems. Henry stored his meager belongings in the garage. James was happy to finally have company. He lived alone since the passing of his wife. Henry noticed some disturbing signs that Kaccha was slowly going downhill.

After a few weeks of moving in, James started dating a divorced women with two boys. James introduced his new girlfriend to Henry. At first, she seemed very sweet and kind but as the relationship progressed Henry started noticing traits of her real personality. James was too much in love to notice.

James was happy again. He was starting a new job, he was in love, so what could go wrong. Poor Henry he was convinced he was born on the wrong side of the moon or if he was cursed by someone or the type that bad luck follows you everywhere you go. He could not catch a break.

After three months of romance, James's girlfriend Charlotte and her two boys aged four- and seven-year-old moved in. James used some storage space at the end of the hallway and turned it to a bedroom for the two boys. It did not take long for some friction to build between charlotte and Henry which caused some concerns for James.

Charlotte was not happy to have Henry and Kaccha in the house. James tried to make her understand, he was a good friend, and he was the one who invited Henry to stay with him.

" I can understand helping a friend but there are limits, you now have a family of your own."

" Charlotte, I cannot toss them out of the house and leave them on the sidewalk. He has nowhere to go."

" And why should that be your problem?"

Henry walked out of the bedroom with his head down and said to James that he would look for a place to move. He did not want to come between him and charlotte and lose is friendship. James told him it was not necessary to move. They could work things out and find a solution so that Henry and Kaccha could stay.

Charlotte did not believe in a menage a trois. The situation was causing turmoil between charlotte and James. She let James know, she did not move in with her two boys to be squabbling all the time. Things needed to change she said to James.

" James's things need to change now and I quote, not tomorrow, next week or next month, I mean now."

" I will see what I can do."

" I do not want you to see what you can do, do it."

" Come on charlotte don't be so cold hearted, he is my best friend. He was there for me when I needed him the most."

" Well, your even now, he helped you, you helped him."

Henry walked out of his room and advised James to called 911, Kaccha's condition was getting worse. Kaccha was again admitted to the hospital but this time she was there to stay. Her health did not permit her to go back home, the hospital would be her new home. After calling 911 James addressed the attitude that charlotte was displaying on a daily basis.

" Satisfied now Kaccha is going back to the hospital. Her condition will not allow her to come home. Charlotte where does this attitude come from? I am starting to wonder if I made the right decision for you and your two boys to shack up with me. "

" Was your friend paying for room and board?"

" No, he bought his own groceries."

" So, he is staying here rent free, you see James it is not an attitude problem that I have. I get mad when I see someone taking advantage of a person with a good heart. I call them human sponges. They keep absorbing and give nothing in return."

" It was not like that at all, if you only knew what the poor man has gone through, maybe you would understand and not hang him before being judged. No need for you to worry anymore the last time his wife was admitted to the hospital the doctor told him if she was admitted again to the hospital, she will not come back home."

" What about his stuff?"

" His stuff."

" Yes, is stuff, you just said that he was not coming back, so I am going to turn his room into a nursery for our baby, I am pregnant with your child."

" Pregnant "

" Yes, pregnant honey, how do you feel about that?"

" One thing for sure it is a surprise, since when do you know?"

" Last week, I was waiting for the right moment to tell you."

" I will go see Henry at the hospital, tomorrow night after work to bring him his laptop and ask him what he wants to do with Kaccha's bed.

" Don't forget his stuff in the garage."

" Charlotte please."

The following evening after work James made is way to the hospital to talk to Henry about the bed and his stuff. Henry greeted James with open arms, he apologized for being the fifth wheel in the house and be caught between him and Charlotte.

" Charlotte was using harsh words aimed at me. It's a good thing it was only words or else I would be full of bullet holes."

" Yes, I know, I had a good chat with her about her behavior towards you. She had an announcement for me, she is pregnant with my first child."

" Way to go my friend, I think congratulations are in order, I am happy for you."

" Thanks, I am happy, I will be a dad, how is Kaccha doing, no changes? "

" No, pneumonia again. "

" Henry it might be a bad time to bring this up, what about her bed and your stuff at my place?"

" Why am I not welcomed at your place anymore? One question where did you meet Charlotte?

" Don't be silly, you know the door will always be open for you. I met charlotte at the bowling alley. Did the doctor confirm that Kaccha will not go home anymore?"

" Yes, he did because now we need to monitor her 24/7. I am sad to say but her days are limited. Can you try and sell her bed for me and keep my stuff in your garage for now?"

" Yes of course, well I better get going, take care my friend, if you need something, do not hesitate to call. "

" I will."

When James arrived home from the hospital, charlotte was waiting for him.

" So, what about his stuff?"

" No hello how was your day, no kiss, all you care about right now is getting rid of Henry's stuff. He wants to sell the bed and for now he wants to keep his things in the garage. "

" Really any storage fees?"

" Charlotte this is getting ridiculous; I do not know why but you are obsessed with getting rid of his belongings."

" I do not like having someone who is a stranger to me, to store his stuff in our garage. "

The two young boys asked their mom.

" Mom will it be like when you were going out with 'Norman always arguing and break things when you get mad?"

" So, your mom is in the habit of breaking things."

" Yes, when she is mad, she breaks stuff."

" Alright you two time for bed, go brush your teeth and go to bed."

" Ok mom, good night, James."

" Good night boys, so the cat is out of the bag, you like to break stuff, we need to have a serious talk."

They talked until the wee hours of the morning; in James mind it was a constructive talk. A few days goes by, when James came home from work, charlotte told him, that morning she sold the bed that Kaccha no longer needed and took the money to buy a crib for the baby, a playpen, some wallpaper and some accessories needed for the baby. James was flabbergasted.

" That money was not ours to spend, that money belongs to Henry, how much did you get for the bed?"

" Two thousand dollars."

" You're kidding me right, two thousand dollars, do you know how much a bed like that is worth? Brand new you're looking at twelve thousand dollars, that bed was still worth about seven thousand dollars, do you know that? "

" Well too late now it's sold, and I purchased items for our baby."

" Tomorrow you will bring everything you purchased today back to the store, like I said it is not our money."

" I do not see it that way, he owed you that money for staying here free of charge. "

" You do not understand Henry needs that money and beside he wanted me to sell the bed, so you will bring back to the store all the stuff you bought."

" I will do no such thing, you know why, there is no refund when you return something at the store you get a store credit."

James was thinking, he made a huge mistake to hook up with her. His life will be a disaster, even if they split up, he will have to stay in contact because of his child. He will give Henry the two grand.

James was able to get a small loan from the bank to give the two thousand dollars to Henry. After work he made his way to the hospital to meet Henry, both men shook hands. James was not sure how to approach Henry to let him know, charlotte sold Kaccha's bed for a mere two thousand dollar.

" James are you alright, you seem preoccupied?"

James said to himself

" Well here goes nothing."

" Come on James, tell me what is going on."

" Yes, Henry there is something that I need to tell you and I do not know how to tell you. "

" Come on James, you know me, say what you have to say."

" A few days ago, when I was at work charlotte sold Kaccha's bed for a mere two thousand dollars. "

" you're kidding right?"

" I wish I was."

" The bed was not for her to sell, who gave her the right to sell the bed in the first place? Be careful with that woman my friend. "

" So, I have the money for you."

" Two thousand dollars, that bed was worth a lot more than two grand. Did she sell some of my belongings?"

" No, your belongings are in my garage."

" Did she have any comments with my stuff in your garage?"

" A few."

" You know what James what's done is done, at least she gave you the money from the sale of the bed."

" Not exactly."

" Come again."

" She took the money to go shopping for items we will need when the baby is born. I took a small loan at the bank to repay you."

Henry's temperature was rising and so was his tone of voice.

" Not only she took it upon herself to sell the bed for peanuts, but she also took the liberty to go shopping with my money."

" Please calm down Henry, I have never seen you like this before."

" This is only the second time in my entire life that the top of my head is boiling, you could fry an egg on my head right now."

" I have my doubts that our friendship is going to last, I am trying to make amends here, do you know Henry relationships or friendships gets stronger when both are willing to understand mistakes and forgive each other."

" It all depends on who you're with and who is your friend."

" Believe me Henry, I defended you, she called you a sponge, do you know what that means, she also quoted, the money was mine because you were living at my place for free. I corrected her about her quote."

" A sponge, you know what James, leave her behind and never look back because your future is ahead of you."

" She is the mother of my unborn baby; I cannot leave her behind and abandon my kid he deserves to have a dad."

" James please go before I say something I might regret; I wish you all the luck in the world my friend."

" Here is your money Henry, I truly hope that we can remain friends, you need to understand Henry she will be the mother of my child. Good luck with Kaccha my dear friend. I hope to talk to you soon."

Henry never contacted James again, he did not want to be caught in the middle between the two. Henry also lost his online job. His mistakes and absenteeism were also a problem.

Henry was supposed to be in front of his computer for eight hours a day. Henry needed a code to access the work that needed to be done and access another code at the end of the day. That's how they were able to keep track of the hours Henry worked.

Kaccha's health was starting to go downhill. Henry was trying to console himself that he was doing the best he could, but for him it was not enough. He could have done better. Every day was more and more painful for him to witness the decline of Kaccha's condition.

CHAPTER 12

Every morning, Henry started his day by going to the small chapel located on the second floor of the hospital. Doctor Applebee got to know Henry quite well, so the doctor advised the hospital staff, Henry was allowed to stay with Kaccha 24/7. He could take showers in the staff's dressing room.

Henry lended a hand, help a nurse mop up a mess, running errands, he was very well liked by everyone. One morning the doctor noticed Kaccha did not pee during the night. Kaccha developed a recurrent urinary tract infection. The catheter inserted into the bladder to drain urine was empty.

The doctor was worried, the infection might spread to the blood stream causing sepsis a life-threatening infection of the blood, also causing skin breakdowns, ulcers because the inability to control passage of urine or stools. The wounds are very difficult to heal.

Doctor Applebee explained the situation to Henry, it was a good thing the infection did not have time to spread to the blood stream.

" Is that bad doctor, is it the beginning of the end for my wife?"

" No, it's an infection that is most common on patients like your wife we hooked up another intravenous so we can give her the medication needed to fight the infection. We will have to keep a close eye on her in case the infection makes another unwelcomed visit."

" Will the infections become more frequent?"

" It remains to be seen, that's why I said a little while ago we need to pay more attention to her catheter."

In the hallway stood a woman facing Kaccha's room, she was shaking her head. The doctor walked over to her.

" Can I help you is there something you need?"

" You know doctor it is a shame to spend all that time and money on a dead body. "

Henry intervened

" I beg your pardon madam she is not a dead body."

" Look at her she is a vegetable, do her a favor and pull the plug."

" She is not a vegetable she is my wife, and she is a human being."

" Used to be."

" Nurse please take this patient back to her room and make sure she does not make her way over here again."

" Yes doctor, come with me please."

" What a bimbo, she is a few bricks short of a load. That reminds me is the lady that used to walk the hallways and say there was a cure for cancer is she still around?"

" No, she was released from the hospital about a month ago and no need to worry about this lady. Henry, we will make sure she does not come over to bother you again. I have to go take care of other patients, see you later Henry."

" Yes and thank you. "

The words the lady said where churning nonstop in his brain. He was anxious for that little mouse to stop turning the wheel. He started questioning himself if he was doing the right thing for Kaccha. The little mouse must have taken a break because he came back to his senses.

She is alive, she can feel things, what was I thinking doubting myself. Back up the truck Henry and get that nonsense out of your head.

Comments coming from that crazy lady should not have such an effect on me. Come on man get it together, stay focused, Kaccha needs me. The one thing that really bothered Henry was Kaccha could feel pain. You can tell when she does, but the nurses are quick to administer her some pain medicine.

I need to go for a walk to clear my head before I end up in a straight jacket. My stress level goes up every day. The only thing keeping Henry going was Kaccha or else he would have given up a long time ago. Every morning in the small chapel, Henry is asking God to not take her away. Although she is confined to a bed, I still want to see her, be by her side every day.

" Dear god as long as her heart beats and pumps blood in her veins, she is warm to the touch. You cannot imagine the love that I have for my precious Kaccha. I adore her and cherish every day that I am by her side. Thank you God for bringing Kaccha into my life. Kaccha is my gift of life. I know you need good souls but please let her stay with me for a while longer. I will be forever in your debt. I do not want to be alone. Alone is a lonely place to be. Amen. "

Henry would always try to put on a happy face. He did not want anybody to feel sorry for him because everyone is living their day to day lives with hidden demons in their hearts waiting to be let loose. The doctor took Henry to a room where they could be alone so they could talk in private.

" Henry, have you noticed the color of your wife's skin lately?"

" To be honest no."

" Take a walk to her room take a real close look at her skin, come back, tell me what you see."

Henry made his way to the room and took a very close look at Kaccha's skin. He did not like what he saw, he made his way back to the doctor.

" Her skin is cracking."

" It's called skin breakdowns and ulcers because of her inability to control passage of urine or stools. The wounds are very difficult to heal

" What docs that mean doctor, she is on her final leg, can she still feel pain?"

" No, she is not on her final leg, but her condition is getting worse and yes she can still feel pain, we give her some medication to ease the pain."

" Is she always in pain? That's a question that never crossed my mind to ask you."

" No, she is not constantly in pain."

" How can you tell?"

" Believe me we know when she is in pain."

" I have been told several times now, I should, like they say pull the plug and end her suffering. I cannot decide for her. What gives me the right to end her life. It's like committing murder. No one as the right to take a life even their own by committing suicide, although it's their own lives they are committing murder."

" It does make sense what you just said, I never thought of it that way. Gotta, go I have patients waiting for me."

One morning Henry was at the cafeteria having breakfast when a man joined him at his table.

" Henry am I right?"

" Yes, and you are?"

" You don't recognize me, the nerdy kid with glasses. Richard."

" Richard is that really you?”

Henry paused for a few seconds

" You look good, I did not recognize you."

" Surprise, surprise my friend, after high school I ditched the glasses for contact lenses, while in college I started pumping iron, look at me now, if only the bullies from high school could see me today, their jaws might drop down to the floor. "

" Well good for you, in what line of work are you in?"

" Computer graphics, I design websites and you Henry what do you do for a living?"

" School teacher."

" School teacher wow man you need to have a lot of patience to become a school teacher. Teaching a class of hoodlums. If you don't mind my asking, what are you doing here today are you sick?"

Henry took the time to explain to Richard, from start to finish the reason why he was at the hospital.

" Oh my god Henry are you serious, you're kidding me, right? "

" Believe me, I wish a was."

" Oh my god Henry, I am so sorry to hear that, so sorry my friend, so sorry, I am here today with my dad because of a mild bladder infection. I was thinking it's the end of the world because my father is not feeling well. I do not know how you do it man I really don't. "

" You do not have a choice, if you go down, your sick sibling will also go down. Believe me is not easy. "

" I can well imagine, one question Henry, have you lost faith in God?"

" That's a hard question to answer, yes and no."

" My dad must be out of the examination room by now, it was nice talking to you, be brave and take care till next time and oh yes. A few of us from our class, we are talking to organize a class reunion. Would you be in if we do?"

" No, I don't think so, but thanks for asking and if you do have one send my regards to everyone attending, can you do that for me?"

" Well of course it will be my pleasure to do that for you. So long my friend."

Henry finished his breakfast and hurried back upstairs to rejoin his wife. Once seated beside Kaccha. Henry was thinking why did it have to happen to us, we were not doing anything wrong or causing any harm to anyone, we were minding our own business.

We were both madly in love, cherishing every moment of our daily lives. A bright future ahead of us. My former schoolmates might plan a night of fun with a class reunion. That's what life is supposed to be, on that fateful day, when Henry received that dreaded phone call that Kaccha was badly hurt. His whole life came tumbling down, smashing to a thousand pieces.

He was in total shock when he finally arrived at the hospital for the first time and walked in the hospital room and saw Kaccha with all the tubes going in and out of her. He almost fainted. He took a few steps backwards closed his eyes, walked back in the room. He kept his eyes shut for a few minutes, afraid to open his eyes, wishing it was only a nightmare.

" Ok, ok, I need to stop torturing myself, I have to stop revisiting the past and especially the dark days since the accident. I need to flush my mind. Push the fast forward button instead of the rewind button. Mom and dad, if you are both watching over me, please help me, I am all alone in this crazy world we live in. I do not know what to do, where to turn, I am lost in my own brain. Please someone help me please. "

When the doctor stepped in the room, Henry was crying, the doctor suggested to Henry that he should walk away for a couple of hours, get some fresh air, go for a walk in the park, go and enjoy a nice meal at a restaurant. Henry looked at the doctor, nodded his head in approval and headed for the elevator.

The fresh air was nice but the walk in the park for Henry was a big mistake. Everybody was enjoying the beautiful sunshine, young couples walking by pushing baby strollers. Couples holding hands smiling, kids with their dogs. Henry lowered his head looking at the ground. He was spaced out when he noticed a pair of feet in front of him. He looked up; a priest was standing in front of him.

" Can I sit down?"

" Yes, father make yourself at home, it won't be long now that a park bench will be my home. "

" What makes you say that sir?"

" You really do not want to know, if I start talking, we will be here until the sun rises tomorrow morning."

" I have nowhere else to go. Is there something I can help you with?"

" Well father what would you say that I have lost faith in my religion."

" Why is that?"

Henry looked at him shook his head and proceeded at telling him his life's story finishing with these words.

" Please do not tell me, God works in mysterious ways. That's all hogwash, if he does work in mysterious ways, he is doing it all wrong or his ways does not make any sense. No offence father."

" None taken wow quite the story."

" It's not a story father it is the truth, if you want proof, take a walk with me to the hospital so you can witness it for yourself. Oh yes one more thing I applied for EI, and it was denied because I quit my job as a school teacher and fired from my online job. I have no income."

" I am sorry Henry it came out the wrong way, what I meant was."

" I know what you meant father, I am sorry, but do you understand where I am coming from. My wife is dying, I have no job, no money no home and I am alone, there is a population of over five billion people on this earth and I am alone. I guess when Kaccha is gone I will pan handle to survive. I saved just enough money to give her a decent funeral."

" Do you pray Henry."

" Yes, every morning in the little chapel at the hospital."

" I am confident when your wife is gone, you will be able to pull yourself together and get on with your life."

" I don't think so. She is my world, without her there is no world. You know father another saying that I do not believe in is when they say time heals everything that's nonsense it helps you cope, some scars never heal. Well, I better get back to the hospital, I was only supposed to be gone for a few hours."

" But Henry, you need to listen to what I have to say."

" Don't bother father you will be wasting your time."

Henry walks away the priest said to himself

" What a poor soul, I hope he makes it."

When Henry returned to the hospital the doctor was in the room

" So, Henry did it help?"

" Not one bit. It made it worse, sitting on a park bench, everybody around me was happy, enjoying life no one paid any attention to me except for a priest. I am devastated, I am angry with life, I cannot absorb it anymore and keep hoping that tomorrow will be better."

" Henry, do you want me to make an appointment with a therapist for you."

" No thank you, talking to a therapist will not change anything, I will leave her, or his office and reality is going to hit me in the face. I am tired of being hit in the face, after a while it hurts. I have all the pain that I can take right now. A therapist is only a band-aid solution. I now feel bitter and resent what has happened to us. Why could we not have a taste of the good life like everybody else? I just want to be left alone please, no more pep talks, no more suggestions, no one can understand the way I feel, our lives taken away from us."

" Boy Henry what a change in your attitude."

" Well sorry for being human, I am fed up. You take for example, the thugs and cutthroats in this world get to live a better life than me, a law-abiding citizen. When people say patience is a virtue, you will see everything will be fine, just wait and see. I am waiting but I still do not see anything positive. For me now the way that I see it, things are going backwards instead of forward. I was once told Henry do not look back on things, your future is ahead of you. Ya right."

" I will see you later Henry."

When the doctor stepped out of the room, that's when Henry realized he was a changed man, with all the stress and the weight on his shoulders was bringing him down. He was at the point he could kiss the floor, that's how low he was.

He needed to apply the brakes, change direction or else he would end up in a dead-end street with nowhere else to go but backwards and that's something he did not want to do. He was physically and emotionally drained, nothing left in the tank. For him it was now a waiting game. He leaned back in his chair and in no time he was asleep.

The next morning, he was trying to make sense of it all but was not able to do so. He needed to remain calm because if he gets aggressive or a torn in everybody's side, they will show him the door and not let him in again. He said to himself

" Be strong no more outburst, no more meltdown, I will only make things worse for me and everybody else."

The nurses and doctors were all doing the best they could under the circumstances. The hospital staff was kind to him, and he did not want to over welcome is stay. Every day the nurses would take turns to bring Henry a lunch from home. When the doctor walked in the room, Henry apologized for his behavior.

" No worries my friend, we all need to blow off some steam once in a while or else we will all crash and burn."

" Thank you doctor for accepting my apology, I will try to not do it again."

" Henry, I hate telling you this, Kaccha's condition is now fragile, I am afraid one more infection or one more bout with pneumonia will be critical she might not pull through. I want to prepare you for the worst but hope for the best."

" I understand, I have heard that quote way too many times in the past few months. I am aware it's only a question of time. I say I am ready, but I guess I will never be one hundred percent ready. Sometimes we think we are prepared but when the time comes, we fall to pieces. "

You want your sibling to end their suffering, but you still want to hang on to them as long as possible. Henry was hoping he was well prepared, but he knew in his heart his whole world will come tumbling down. Then the domino effect gets in motion. You cry, you grieve, make funeral arrangements. Relatives that you haven't seen in years show up.

" My condolences she/he was a good caring person. He was one of my favorite one in the family."

Really their favorite, but it's been decades since they talked to each other. Listen to hypocrites. For some they really don't want to go to the funeral, they think it's a obligation. They show up at the cemetery, they are like a cat on hot bricks, they leave before the last word is said.

Henry was thinking, no need for me to worry about that, I have no one, I am alone. All alone. He was trying to think of a plan to put in motion when Kaccha is gone. He could not think straight, he was always drawing a blank. After lunch Henry was sleeping in his chair when James paid him a visit. He did not want to wake him up. He put a bag on the small table beside the bed and walked away.

When Henry opened his eyes, he noticed the bag on the table. He inquired if one of the nurses had forgotten a bag on the table. Negative answers, so Henry looked in the bag. There was a note along with some new clothes and an envelope with some cash in it. Henry read the note.

" Henry, I am so, so, so sorry that our friendship as gone sour. I was stuck between a rock and a hard place. The fact that I was going to be a dad was overwhelming for me. Charlotte is now seven months pregnant; I cannot wait to be a dad. As a friend I care about you. Sometimes life throws us a curve ball and we need to change our way of thinking and doing things we are in the process of moving to Tampa Bay Florida. I know that you need new clothes and a little spare cash. Please accept this token of appreciation for what we used to call our friendship. I wish you all the best my dear friend. I was blessed to have a good friend like you. .... James."

Henry did not know what to make of it. He squeezed the bag to his stomach, tears started trickling down is face. He took the clothes out of the bag, two brand new pair of pants, two dress shirts and five hundred dollars in cash in the envelope. Henry also spotted his meager belongings in the corner of the room.

" I guess there are still good people left in this world."

Henry went in the bathroom to clean himself up, changed into his new clothes, discarded his old clothes in the trash. For Henry it was refreshing wearing new clothes. The extra money will come in handy. God bless you my dear friend and take care of yourself. One of the nurses spotted Henry coming down the hallway.

" Well, well Henry look at you, you look good in your new clothes. I was wondering who was the handsome dude walking in the hallway. Good for you."

" Thanks, but I have been wearing the same underwear for I should say close to two months now."

" Ok now I know where that foul stench is coming from, just joking Henry."

" I am not joking, yes I am joking."

" Good you found your sense of humor; it was nonexistent the past couple of weeks."

" Yes, I know, but you know what, an act of kindness can sure go a long way to boost your morale."

" It sure does, it's the little things in life that matter the most. Hey ladies, look at this handsome man standing next to me."

Henry was the recipient of cat calls, some whistling. It did Henry some good it made him realize he was still able to smile. His smile was not gone after all, the smile was only taking a break. Henry disappeared for a few minutes; he came back with flowers in a vase.

" Here ladies some nice flowers to show you, my gratitude. All of you make me feel like I am part of the family."

One of the nurses took the vase added water and put the flowers in the vase and put the vase on the counter and gave Henry a hug.

" Incidentally Henry there are not too many ladies working on this floor, if you know what I mean?"

The nurses responded.

" Hey, speak for yourself you are the worst one in the bunch."

Everybody was laughing when the doctor stepped out of the elevator.

" You look like a happy bunch, what is going on here? Is there a party and I was not invited? Wow Henry you look mighty spiffy in your new clothes. Are they giving you a hard time? If they are my friend, no salary increases for the next two years for you ladies.

" There's your proof we are all ladies here, am I right doctor?"

" Sure, you are, a fine bunch of ladies."

" To tell you the truth doctor, I was fighting them off, they all wanted their fifteen minutes of fame in the broom closet with me."

" You should all be ashamed trying to take advantage of this poor man, if I come in with new clothes tomorrow morning, am I going to get the same reception."

" Heck no doctor, we all know what you're carrying in your pants, we go spy on you when you take a shower before going home."

" Boy the hospital must have been hard pressed to hire a bunch of hooligans like yourselves, now back to work you bunch of slackers."

A week later Kaccha was in a deep coma. The doctor again took Henry aside to talk to him.

" I am afraid Henry that Kaccha will never regain consciousness, she can be in a coma for a week, a month we do not really know."

" Can she still hear us when we talk?"

" Yes, she can."

" I know what your next question is doctor, the answer is no. As long as her heart beats she is still alive."

" Yes, I know Henry, what I was going to tell you, we need to transfer her upstairs to the ninth floor, there is a special unit that can monitor patients 24/7. A nurse is always present in the room, it's a room with four beds, it will not be as private as it is here, but I do not have a choice to transfer her. Hospital protocol."

" No, it's ok doctor it's all right I understand. "

" We will transfer her upstairs the day after tomorrow. They need a couple of days to get everything ready for her transfer. I will still be her doctor. Do not worry she will be in capable hands."

" I know she will be in good hands, will they let me stay with her?"

" Yes, they will, when Kaccha is transferred upstairs, everything will be ready for the both of you."

" You guys are out of this world when it comes to accommodate a patient's siblings. You do not get this kind of service at a five-star hotel."

When the time came to transfer Kaccha, Henry made is way to the flower shop, purchased a vase, nice flowers and a thank you card. In which he wrote

" Thank you so much for all what you have done for me and especially feed me. I asked God for help, he sent me angels in which I had the privilege to get to know and love, all of you will always be in my heart. The compassion is incredible, the hospital is blessed to have all of you part of their team."

P.s. "you are all good-looking ladies. .... Henry."

Henry put the flowers in the vase and put the vase on the counter at the nurse's aid station. One of the nurses read the back of the card out loud, everyone was holding back tears.

Henry also wrote on a piece of paper " My dear angels......, I was so blessed to have a wonderful group of nurses to take care of Kaccha. I am going upstairs floor nine which means Kaccha will be closer to heaven, without your love and compassion, all of your lovely smiles, I would probably be in the looney bin. Every one of you have a piece of my heart, which I will always carry with me and when I am feeling blue, I will put my hand on my heart and feel the compassion from everyone of you, to help me to get back on track. I asked God for help, and he sent angels and all of you will never lose you place in my heart, my precious ladies.......Henry. "

They decided to organize a raffle in his honor. The raffle was a success. They raised nine hundred dollars with the raffle and the winner donated is winnings. For a grand total of one thousand two hundred fifty dollars.

They summoned Henry to go to the nurse's aid station. When Henry was handed the envelope, he could not believe his eyes when he opened the envelope. One of the nurses mentioned, the expression on Henry's face was priceless. She could see the joy, the love and gratitude. Henry was crying.

" If I keep on crying the way that I am now, I won't have to pee for a week. I am at a loss for words. This is incredible, how many times did I say to myself you are alone in this big world of ours, but I was wrong, I have a tremendous family standing in front of me. You guys are the best and will always be the best. No group will never be able to hold a candle compared to all of you."

Cake was served, a lot of hugs, tears, laughter, kind words all mixed together in the same bowl. A bowl of human kindness and compassion. A bowl that is very hard to find now days.

Henry thanked God to surround him with human angels when he needed them the most. He knew Kaccha's days were numbered. Every night he would reluctantly fall asleep, for him every morning was one less morning, he would wake up next to her.

When Kaccha was comfortable in her new room, it did not take long for everyone to warm up to Henry. It was on everybody's mind; it was not fair for good people like Kaccha and Henry to have the rug pulled from under their feet. It's a darn shame.

So many good years ahead of them they could have enjoyed. The love Henry has for Kaccha is indescribable, it's a love so deep that you cannot find on any street corner. You only see that kind of stuff in movies. A lot of women would kill to have a man like Henry with all that love to give.

One morning, Doctor Applebee took Henry aside again, Henry was well aware when the doctor took him aside to talk to him, it was not good news.

" Henry by now you must know why I need to talk to you in private. Her oxygen level is starting to be a problem, she now needs a lot of oxygen for her to breathe. The reason is we have to give her bigger doses of the medication to clear her lungs. That means her heart is weaker. What does not help she contracted pneumonia four or five times. Her limbs are now limp brought on by the inability to move. You know by increasing her daily doses of medication what it does to a human anatomy. We will do everything we can for her, to keep her comfortable and for your sake Henry and keep her here with you as long as we can. I want you to be prepared Henry. There is no time frame for her to leave us, you know that don't you? I hope for your sake that you do know what is coming. "

" Yes, I do know, and I cannot say enough I do not know how to say thank you, because thank you is not enough. Like I said before for what you have all done for me."

" We try our best every day we do not always succeed, but we try."

" I know you do; I see it every day."

When the doctor was gone, Henry was looking at Kaccha wondering how many more days, he will be able to look at Kaccha in her bed. A life without her by his side will be very difficult. He was not sure if he will be able to cope or ever live a normal life again. What will he do? Where will he go? How is he going to survive? Without Kaccha he will never be the same man again.

Another six weeks went by before the doctor again took Henry aside. this time Henry said.

" Oh, oh."

" Oh, oh yes indeed Henry. We are down to only a matter of days or even hours. We cannot really tell. We do not know how long her heart will be able to."

One of the nurses ran out of Kaccha's room.

" Please come quick."

The doctor rushed into the room, Kaccha was choking with her own secretion. Thanks to the quick reaction from the doctor. They were able to clean the tube, again after a mere five hours the tube was blocked again. The doctor advised Henry to say his final words to her.

" My darling wife, I will always love you, I am happy for you, the pain will be gone, and you will be on your way to heaven, I am devastated by the thought of you leaving me. My sweet little angel, when you came into my life it made me believe in angels. This will probably be my last poem that I recite to you, so please make sure to listen to every word that I am about to tell you."

" My darling wife, the love of my life, you will always be in my heart, we will never be apart, we became one in loving presence together, in love we come to heaven forever, like two doves we sing and danse, love of queen and king, our love will last, I dream of a woman clothed in white, her hair is fine like that of an olden wife, you whisper love through the wings of life, rivers of love flow to my heart and my spirit ascends, I grow embraced by heavenly lights, then grow rays of warmth and light, every word comes from the bottom of my heart."

" I do not want you to go. I know, I am selfish for wanting you to stay but I cannot help it. My love for you is so deep for you. My love for you is deeper than the universe."

Henry was trying to stay composed, pacing the floor. He decided to get comfortable beside Kaccha's bed and not move an inch. He wanted to be with her when the time comes. One of the nurses will stay in the room with Henry.

He did not want Kaccha to leave this world alone and surrounded by strangers. Henry would fall asleep only to wake up every thirty minutes to check on Kaccha. He was true to his word; he would only leave for a minute to go to bathroom.

The nurses were looking in his direction with tears in their eyes. In all their years of working at the hospital, never did they see such devotion, compassion, and love for your significant other and they will probably never see it again. Henry is one in a billion. In the morning when the doctor walked in the room, Henry was leaning on the side of the bed sleeping.

" Henry wake up, you should sleep on the cot next to the bed."

" No, I cannot do that, I want to feel her last heartbeat. I sleep with one of my hands on her heart. If I am asleep when she goes, my hand will feel her last heartbeat, she will know that I am here with her."

" Her oxygen level as dropped to a dangerous level, her heart is fading, her lungs will not be able to handle all that liquid."

Just then, one of the machines hooked up to Kaccha started beeping, the doctor looked at Henry to let him know, one of her lungs collapsed.

" Henry it's only a matter of hours. It will be a miracle if she makes it through the night."

Henry grabbed her hand.

" I will not let go sweetheart. "

A few hours later Kaccha was gone.

" No please sweetheart not yet please give me one more day, please only one more day, please, one more day."

One of the nurses grabbed his hands.

" It's ok Henry, she is now with God. Come with me please."

" No, I do not want to leave her, I want to stay with her a little longer please."

Henry was talking to her, stroking her hair, squeezing her hands. The doctor confirmed that she passed away.

" Come with me Henry."

" Why? Kaccha needs me."

" Henry please come with me, we will go see a counselor."

Two workers from the morgue put a blanket over Kaccha's head and started wheeling her away.

" Hold it where are you taking my wife?"

" They are taking her downstair in the basement."

" No doctor, they cannot bring her there, that's where they bring dead people, I will not allow it. "

The nurse approached Henry with a needle in her hands, Henry started backing up.

" I know what's in that needle, I do not want it. It's going to put me to sleep. No time to sleep Kaccha needs me."

Henry ran down the hallway, grabbed, pushed the two men away, who were bringing Kaccha to the morgue. Henry grabbed her bed and was making his way back to her room.

" You cannot take her away. She is my wife, I want her to stay here, they take very good care of her here, she is not going anywhere. "

The nurse approached Henry from behind, buried a needle in his arm. Henry looked at her.

" It's not over she is not gone for real, what if you made a mistake and she is still alive, mistakes like that do happen, I saw that on television. Right doctor?"

" There is no mistake Henry, I am truly sorry for your lost."

The effect of the needle started kicking in, Henry sat down in the chair and fell asleep. One of the nurses said.

" Poor man, so much more love to give, I don't think he will ever be able to recover."

When Henry woke up, he was asking where was Kaccha, was she in a different room? The nurse painfully reminded him that Kaccha passed away earlier in the day.

" I was not dreaming, it was not my worse fear, my worst nightmare she is really in heaven."

Henry was pale as a ghost; he was sitting in his chair crying his eyes out. The priest tried to console him. No word could describe his sorrow. The doctor advised Henry, the way he was feeling, it would be best for him to be hospitalized for a few days. Henry would not hear of it. He needed to be strong for Kaccha.

" Henry it is a known fact, people die as a result of a broken heart, you need to be careful and take care of yourself."

" Why Kaccha is gone, if I die, I will be in heaven with her."

" Henry just think for a minute, would Kaccha want you to be strong, continue your journey, find happiness again while she waits for you in heaven. She is probably looking down at you right now."

Henry was able to compose himself and finally accepted the fact that Kaccha was gone. The doctor let Henry sleep one last time in the room, he advised the nurses to keep an eye on him. When morning came the priest wanted to discuss funeral arrangements with him. Henry wanted Kaccha to be cremated. The funeral director was waiting to hear from Henry.

Henry found the courage to make is way and talk to the funeral director. They proceeded on making all the necessary arrangements. The director took Henry downstairs, so he could say a final goodbye.

Henry removed part of the blanket that was covering her face. He grabbed Kaccha by the waist, lifted Kaccha in a sitting position and her head on his shoulder. He was running his fingers through her hair, kissing her neck.

" No Kaccha come back it is not too late for you to come back, I can't let go, please just one more day. "

The funeral director took Henry aside to tell him to say his final goodbye. Henry responded that he could not say goodbye. Henry was finally able to compose himself and said his final goodbye, kissed her on the cheek and covered her face. He prayed for a few minutes, followed the director upstairs for a recap of the arrangement

" To make sure Mr. Engelbrecht that we have everything in order, neither one of you has any family members coming to the funeral only a few friends. The funeral is scheduled for the day after tomorrow two pm and you want to bring the urn home with you."

Henry made his way back to the hospital to pick up a few personal items and let everybody know the time and date of the funeral. Only one nurse was at the nurse's desk. Henry walked over.

" Can you please do me a favor, can you tell everybody goodbye for me, I will miss all of you, I feel as if I am leaving home."

" I sure will Henry, we will miss you. Please take care of yourself.".

Henry made is way to the elevator with his meager possessions, took a deep breath. After leaving the hospital, Henry checked into a bed and breakfast costing eighty-five dollars a day. He sat on the bed to count the money in his pocket.

The funeral for Kaccha was paid for in advance. He counted a grand total of one thousand seven hundred eighty-two dollars Henry needed to find a way to make money and in a hurry. Henry did not bother to try to locate Kaccha's parents, the same for Lucas and Mrs. Moore.

Only eight of the hospital staff were able to attend the funeral because of the work schedule. It was a sad moment, but Henry was happy to see them. Hugs, kisses, goodbyes were said, and everyone went their own way. He said to himself it would be the last time, Henry would see his friends. unfortunately, Henry will see his friends when he is admitted to the hospital for his final days.

Henry was given permission to use the computer at the bed and breakfast, Henry typed his resume and searching online for a job.

CHAPTER 13

Everyday Henry was pounding the pavement to try to find a job. Most jobs he applied for. He was hearing the same statement from employers, you are over qualified. No school was hiring teachers because of the cutback in funding by the government. Henry's cashflow was dwindling down.

He started knocking on doors asking homeowners if they had chores or work that needed to be done. On an average day Henry would make between sixty to eighty dollars a day. Some days a little more, some days a little less. Henry was earning peanuts, but it was Henry's lifeline.

One day when returning to the bed and breakfast, he was robbed for the money he earned that day by a couple of young men. Henry only had forty-three dollars in his pockets, he pleaded with them not to take the money, he needed the money to buy food. They laughed at him. One of the young men punched him in the face. Henry could hear them laughing while running away.

Henry was tempted to falsify is resume. He was reluctant because of the consequences, the danger of being caught. He would be committing fraud to get a job. He would be looking at jail time. He started thinking maybe jail was not such a bad idea, three meals a day a warm bed. Kaccha would never approve and would be disappointed with him.

Every day he was out there trying to earn money. He came up with a new strategy, find work during the day and panhandle at night. He made sure not to invade the spot of another homeless man. He did not make much money panhandling but every dollar counts.

One evening a nurse from the hospital was driving home, she spotted Henry, she was not sure if it was him or not. She could not stop to verify if it was him due to the traffic. The following night she slowly drove by to get a better glimpse of the man who was panhandling.

She could clearly see, it was Henry, again she could not stop because of the traffic. When coming home from work the following evening, she parked her car in a vacant parking lot, about half a block from where Henry was sitting begging for money. She walked over, stood in front of Henry, he lifted his head, he was about to get up and go home in shame.

" Henry it's me Gloria, you do remember me right.? From the hospital, please do not go. Why don't we go for a cup of coffee and something to eat, I have not eaten dinner yet, I am starving. Please come and have dinner with me.

" Yes, I know who you are, I am so ashamed that you had to see me like this."

" Everything you did for your wife, you should not be ashamed, I am sorry that I could not attend the funeral because of work. Now get up and let's go."

She grabbed Henry by the hand, crossed the street, walked a short distance to a nice little diner.

" Henry I am happy to see you, we were wondering at the hospital how you were doing."

" Please do me a favor Gloria, don't tell them the way you found me please. I cannot find a job in my field of work. To cut cost, the California government cut thirty thousand teaching jobs. I cannot even get a toe nail in the door. The teacher's union makes sure the state of California does not hire a teacher that is not in the teacher's union, so if a teaching position becomes available, one of the laid off teachers will get the job."

" I promise I will not say a word."

" Every job I apply for I hear the same story over and over you are too qualified. I even applied a few places for tutoring kids at home, again the laid off teachers get the jobs."

" that's a shame a well-educated man like yourself cannot land a job it does not make any sense."

" I still have a little bit of pride left, as I was saying I cannot get a teaching job, every job interview I go same story over qualified. I knock on doors, ask the owners of the house if there is work that I can do for them. I do not make much, but it helps me survive. At some point I was thinking to change the information on my resume, but the consequences are too great if I get caught, jail time, with a criminal record no company would want to hire me."

" It's a shame, such a waste of a good soul, so well educated, a man that has so much to give but not given the chance to do so."

" Thank you."

Henry enjoyed a nice dinner with Gloria, Henry was happy to spend time with a friend, although it was only for a few hours.

" I am trying to find a cheaper place to live, but it's like walking barefoot on broken glass without getting any shards in your feet. It's impossible to find. I live at a bed and breakfast place that cost eighty-five dollars a day. "

" I do not want to take the wind out of your sails Henry, but I do not think you will be able to find anything cheaper, not around here that's for sure."

Before leaving Gloria gave Henry fifty dollars. Henry did not want to take the money.

" You have a family to raise, keep the money for your kids."

" Henry it is no time to be stubborn, take the money, I have no budget constraints, so please put it in your pocket. "

" Ok, thank you."

As Gloria was about to leave she turns towards Henry, gave him a hug, a kiss on the cheek, paused for a minute.

" Henry this time of year my uncle needs a helper to bring in the crops. Would that be something that might interest you? If yes, I can give him a call."

" That would be great, thank you."

I will call him right now, if he is not home, I will leave him a message to call me back. It's ringing.

" Hi uncle Trevor, it's Gloria, how are you?......Yes, everything is good........ My mom and dad are ok....... Ok I will tell them to call you. The reason for my call uncle Trevor, first of all it's to say hi and do you still need a man to help you with the crops? ......Yes good, I have a friend who is looking for work. His name is Henry...... Yes, I understand I will tell him what is involved...........yes, he is standing next to me. Henry the job will be for a three-week period, if needed room and board provided, the work will be from dawn to dusk, makes it for very long days. Twenty bucks an hour. What do you think?"

" I will take it."

" He says he will take it.........In ten days......No he does not have a car......I will give him a ride it will give me the chance to visit....... Yes, see you then, thank you Uncle Trevor I am sure you will not be disappointed in his work. Love you bye. "

" Thank you Gloria, this job is really going to help me."

" My pleasure what friends are for, Henry I do not want to poke my nose where it does not belong. Can I ask you what is in the tote bag, you keep so close to you?"

" It's Kaccha, the urn is always with me, so we can still be close."

" How sweet, the urn follows you everywhere."

" Yes. I once made her a promise that I will always by her side no matter what."

" That is so sweet. Henry here is the deal; you start working for my uncle in ten days. Nice coincidence I am not working that day. I will pick you up here at eight o'clock in the morning, it's a one-hour drive on a country road, nice scenery to look at. Your salary includes room and board. He will pay you cash, I hope you do not mind. "

" No not at all, I prefer it that way."

" You might put on a few pounds on that scrawny body of yours. My aunt is a terrific cook. There is always more than enough if you want seconds."

" That's good. "

" I have to run, see you in ten days."

" You betcha. Kaccha did you hear the conversation. I start a job on a farm for about a month. Twenty dollars an hour with free room and board. What do you think of that? Let's go home, you must be tired after such a long day. I know I am."

 Henry continued his daily and night routine up to the day when Gloria picked him up to go to the farm. Henry was anxiously waiting for Gloria. Henry jumped in the car, put his stuff in the backseat.

" Is that all your stuff?"

" Yes."

" Ok."

" I took my stuff with me, if I wanted to keep my things at the bed and breakfast it would have cost me the same amount that I am paying now to keep my stuff in my room.

Henry enjoyed the ride, the scenery. The small talk with Gloria, listening to music from the car radio. He was lost in his thoughts, how life could have been so sweet and wonderful for him and Kaccha.

" Day dreaming again about you and Kaccha. We have arrived at my uncle's farm."

When Gloria and Henry arrived at the farm, they were greeted by her aunt named Sophie. Gloria and her aunt embraced.

" This my aunt Sophie."

" Nice to meet you, Henry."

" it's a pleasure meeting you ma am."

" Now, now Henry around here we are on a first name basis."

" Where is Uncle Trevor?"

" He is in the garage doing repairs on the tractor."

Henry was shown to his room, it did not take him long to settle in. He went back downstairs where he met Trevor. Henry was served breakfast when done with breakfast off he went to work.

Gloria stayed for a little while. She made her aunt aware of Henry's misfortunes. Midafternoon she was on her way home. Coming back to the house, Henry noticed that Gloria was gone.

Trevor and Henry washed up for dinner, Henry took his place at the dinner table, while having dinner. Trevor was making small talk.

" Where were you born Henry?"

" South Africa."

" You're a long way from home."

" I was two years old when my parents moved to the U.S."

" So, Trevor, did Henry make the cut. He won't have to spend the first two nights working to catch up on his work."

Henry looked at her. Is she serious or joking? He hoped she was joking, working day and night was not part of the deal.

" I am only joking. But if you need to work at night you can sleep in the barn."

" Will you stop it Sophie, you're going to scare him away and I will be stuck with no helper. Do not mind her, since banging her head the other night, she doesn't make any sense when she talks."

" The only time I did not make any sense was when I married you."

All through dinner, they were throwing insults at one and another.

" So, Henry who do you think won the insult competition? Remember you have to work with me tomorrow. "

" You Trevor."

" That's not fair you bribed him."

After dinner Henry went upstairs to his room to watch some television. In a matter of minutes, he was asleep. Henry was holding his own until he broke his hand while working. He tripped and fell on the barn's cement floor. He was not a happy camper to say the least.

" Four days on the job and I injure myself."

Trevor took him to the hospital where they put a cast on his hand. Henry would be out of action for six weeks. He came back to the farm to gather his things; Trevor drove him back to the bed and breakfast. When the time came to remove the cast Henry, took it upon himself to remove it. No more hospitals for him. He had his fair share of hospitals.

Henry wanted to rent his old room. It was not available, as a matter of fact no rooms available. Henry rented a room at another bed and breakfast which was more expensive at one hundred dollars a day. He was fuming just my luck; he was wondering what he did wrong in his previous life to have such bad luck.

Henry spent his days pan handling; he was pan handling at a different location. He did not want Gloria to know where he was. He was too embarrassed to face her. With only one good hand, there was not much he could do about finding work. No one in their right mind would hire a man with only one good hand.

Henry tried to keep his injured hand hidden. He was not in the mood to answer questions. He was relieved when the cast came off.

Henry always paid for his room at the end of the week. One Friday morning Henry gathered his things. He had no money to pay the amount owing to the owners of the bed and breakfast. Henry hated himself for sneaking out and not pay what he owed. His number one priority was to survive any way possible.

" Kaccha please forgive me for what I have done, I did not have a choice, I hope you understand."

Henry was living from one shelter to another, he would panhandle in different areas. He hated his life, he promised Kaccha he will never give up on life and make the best of it, no matter the situation. Every night he wished to die in his sleep.

The urn was always by his side. Before falling asleep at night, he would take his shoelaces and secure the urn around his arm. If an individual would try to steal the urn while he slept, he could feel it moving and wake him up.

One morning walking to find a spot to sit down and panhandle, he spotted an old, abandoned tool shed in someone's backward. The shed was about a hundred feet from the house. Henry thoroughly inspected the shed, it was not in that bad of a shape, no danger for the roof or walls collapsing on him while sleeping.

He will need to be quiet and vigilant not to be seen or not make any noise in case the home owner or the neighbors alert the authorities to make a complaint about an intruder. He made his way back to the sidewalk made himself as comfortable as possible for the day and kept an eye on the shed to make sure it was really abandoned.

When people would inquire if he was a war veteran and say yes, he could take a break from panhandling for three or four months and still have money left over. When he answers to the individuals put back their five-dollar bill in their wallet and look in their pockets for some change, some have no change and say sorry, I do not have any change and walk away.

Henry cannot lie to people that he is a war veteran; it would be a lack of respect for those who put their lives on the line to protect us. One more thing what if they start asking questions about his service in the military.

After dark Henry quietly made his way to the shed. Earlier in the day when he secretly inspected the shed, on his way back to the sidewalk, he studied the terrain from the road to the shed, to make sure not to trip in the dark and make noise or even hurt himself.

There was a little bit of a light in the shed coming from one of the street lights. It was just enough light to help Henry maneuver in the shed without making any noise. One night he was very happy to be in the shed, heavy rain, and high winds. Henry was a bit cold but dry. The next morning it was still pouring rain, windy. Henry stayed put.

Henry heard a noise coming from underneath a small pile of wood in the corner of the shed. Henry looked both ways before proceeding to the wood pile. After lifting a few boards, Henry spotted a little kitten that took refuge from the elements. Henry took him in his arms fed him and gave him water. He decided to keep the little fellow, he named him tiny.

Henry really enjoyed having tiny for company. He noticed with the little kitten on his lap. More people stopped to pet the cat and put money in his can. For Henry it was a win, win situation, a little partner to keep him company and a little bit more money.

One evening going back to the shed Henry was spotted by one of the neighbors. Henry was settling in for the night when he saw a man with a flashlight coming towards the shed. The man with the flashlight was the property owner. When he saw Henry and his stuff in the corner of the shed.

" Who are you? What are you doing in my shed? I can see you have been here for a while."

" My name is Henry, and this is tiny, yes I have been using the shed as a shelter."

" I am the owner of the property including the shed, who gave you permission to use my shed as a shelter?"

" No one sir, to me sir it looked like an abandoned shed, that nobody was using."

" You took for granted you could use it. I could have you arrested for trespassing."

" Yes, I know."

" Is that an urn?"

" Yes, sir it is. The ashes of my wife are in the urn."

" Why not put the urn in a resting place in the cemetery?"

" Long story, I used to be a school teacher, my wife worked in a lab. She had a bad accident while I was away looking for my sister, she never regained consciousness, she was in a vegetative state until she died. You see sir I made her a promise when we got married, I would always be there for her I would never leave her behind."

" Really."

" Yes, sir I tell you no lies. I loved my wife, I still do so much, I sacrificed everything to be by her side until the day she died. Nobody wants to hire me, always the same answer I am over qualified for the job I applied for. A friend got me a job at her uncle's farm, four days on the job I broke my hand. I have no family, I am alone in this big world of ours, completely alone."

" Sad story if you ask me, why did you not come and knock on my door if it was alright to use the shed?" I see you love animals; you have a little partner there with you."

" Yes, tiny brings me joy every day. I am so sorry sir, you are right, I have no right to use your shed without permission, I will pack my stuff and be out of your way in a few minutes. Come tiny time to pack and go find a new home. I do not have much, I can pay for the time I used your shed sir, like I said I am truly sorry."

Henry reached in his pocket, took out the little money he had to pay the owner. The owner refused the money and gave Henry permission to stay in the shed

" The reason I did not go knock at your door, ask your permission if I could use the shed is because with my luck you would have said no. "

" You seem to be a good man who fell on hard times. I admire what you did to keep your promise to your wife."

" With the urn with me, Kaccha is always by my side."

" Ok well goodnight, Henry, goodnight tiny. Sorry I did not introduce myself; my name is Larry. You were lucky to marry a good woman, me my marriage was a disaster from the start."

Larry lived alone, after a messy divorce, he decided to remain single, no more headaches for him. He was getting used to being single. Henry was crying. He was relieved that Larry let him use the shed.

" Thank you very, very, much for letting me stay."

Every couple of days, Larry would bring Henry some food. Everything was great until one night two homeless men followed Henry to the shed. Henry only noticed the two men when he was about to go in the shed. One of the men said.

" Nice place you got here, do you want to share your place with me and my buddy?"

" No, the owner of the shed let me stay here in one condition, I stay quiet and do not cause any problems, so can you gentlemen please leave."

" What if we want to stay?"

" Go talk to Larry, he is the one who owns the property."

" We do not want to talk to no Larry."

Larry heard the commotion and made his way to the shed,

" Can you gentlemen please leave, we do not want any problems, if you refuse to leave, I will call the cops."

The two men looked at each other, turned around and walked away.

" That's what I was afraid of. Please be more careful, make sure you are not followed one more event like this one, I am afraid you will have to leave."

" I understand, I did not know I was followed until I reached the shed. Sneaky and quiet them two."

" Ok Henry goodnight, remember what I told you. After a difficult lengthy and costly divorce all I want is peace and quiet."

" No worries Larry, I apologize for the inconvenience."

" No need to apologize it was not your fault."

Everyday Henry would keep an eye out for the two men who harassed him for the shed. At night on his way to the shed he would say.

" So far so good."

No trace of the two men since that evening but it did not mean he was going to let his guard down. After a month Henry was thinking they heard and understood the warning from Larry not to come back or face the consequences. Larry invited Henry for a meal and an evening of television, they exchanged stories about the roadblocks and bumps on the road.

" And I was complaining about my divorce. Quite the story my friend. My divorce is nothing compared to your agony."

" Your divorce was not nothing, you struggled for over a year to be able to finalize you divorce. It is the kind of thing that will stay with you, you're going to adapt but not forget. You're a good man Larry, she was crazy not to keep you."

" Oh well maybe someday she will realize the grass might look greener on the other side of the fence, but it's not always the case. If you drive and see a cow pasture stop to take a look, the cows remain on the same side of the fence, they reach for the grass close to the other side of the fence, smart animals. "

" Thanks for the evening, Larry, it was fun, I have not watch television in a very long time."

" Your welcome Henry if my house was bigger and some space that, I was not using, I would let you stay with me, but a small 1-bedroom house, no basement space is limited."

" That's ok, I am comfortable in the shed and again thank you for the fine evening it did the body good."

A few nights later when Henry was making his way back to the shed. The same two men who harassed Henry for the shed were hiding, they jumped Henry by surprise. They punched and kicked him, took his money and the urn. Henry begged them to give him back the urn.

" Please give me back my urn, you can use the shed, I will give you money every day, I beg you please. The ashes of my wife are in the urn. Please don't take it away from me. Please it is the only thing I have left in this world, please."

" Now he is begging, how the tables have turned, we can make a pretty penny selling the urn."

One of the men opened the cover of the urn and turned the urn upside down Henry could see the ashes coming out of the urn, landing on the ground.

Henry cried.

" No, no, no Kaccha."

" Kaccha what a weird name she must have learned to fight young with a name like that. Thanks for the money and the lovely urn, we will be able to sell the urn in no time."

They rough up Henry some more, before leaving, Henry could hear them laughing. Henry crawled over to where the ashes fell, Henry tried to pick up the ashes. He could not do it, the ashes were spread to far apart, and to make things worse there was a small breeze, Kaccha's aches were spread all over the place. Henry did not get up from the ground. Henry was crying

" Kaccha my darling I am so sorry I cannot go on anymore without you, God come get me please. Kaccha I am so sorry, Kaccha come back to me please. Kaccha, Kaccha."

Henry did not get up, he did not move an inch, when Henry was done crying, he fell asleep. The following day he was still on the ground, his little buddy beside him. Because of the tall grass, Henry could not be seen by pedestrians or passing cars.

Larry realized he had not seen or heard from Henry for the past couple of days. He walked over to the shed. The little bit of stuff that belonged to Henry was still in the shed. He decided to go take a walk behind the shed. That's when he saw Henry on the ground in a fetal position, Larry ran over to Henry who was weak and trembling.

" My goodness Henry what happened? Here take my hand it will help you get up."

" The two men who wanted the shed, remember them? They attacked me from behind, beat me, took my money, they took the urn, before leaving they removed the top from the urn, flipped it upside down, spreading Kaccha's aches on the ground."

" Assholes, let's go to the house, get you warmed up a bit and I will take you to the hospital. Stealing the urn, making sure, you could see the aches being spilled on the ground, assholes."

Larry made some coffee, prepared a small lunch for Henry, Larry was deeply saddened to see Henry, a broken man, nothing to live for anymore. Larry went in his bedroom to gather some clothes for Henry.

" Here Henry some dry clothes, they might be too big, but they are dry. Remove the wet clothes and put on dry clothes. When you are done eating your meal, I will bring you to the hospital. You are in very bad shape; you need to see a doctor."

" They took Kaccha she is gone forever, all I want now is for God to come and get me, open the doors of heaven so I can walk inside the house of God and join Kaccha, why this Larry, why. Why did they have to take the urn and again why me?"

" I do not know Henry; I wish I could answer that question."

" I do not want to go to the hospital, I will go back in the shed, fall asleep and never open my eyes again, until I get to heaven."

" Come on Henry you know I cannot let you do that. I am sure Kaccha would want you to keep going."

" Not this way. Do me a favor, this is the first time, I am asking you for a favor, let me go lie down and die, "

" It is not going to happen, not on my watch. Do you want me to feel guilty for the rest of my life because I did not bother to bring you to a hospital? Come on move your ass, get in the truck."

Henry slowly walked to the truck, sat in the passenger's seat, Larry climbed in on the driver's side of the truck, and they were on their way to the hospital. After Henry was admitted to the hospital, the doctor told Larry

" He is suffering from exposure, pneumonia, a lung infection, that man is in a very deep depression, I am no psychiatrist, but I don't think he will be able to recover from the depression, what happened to the poor guy for him to be in this poor and mental condition?"

" Very long story, poor man bad luck follows him everywhere, it's been raining on his parade since grade school. Losing his parents at a very young age. Poor Henry the cards have been stacked against him from birth. You could write a book about his misfortunes."

" Once he recovers from his ailments, I will keep him here to have him evaluated by a psychiatrist. I could bet one month of my salary that Henry will stay in the hospital under psychiatric care."

" Great, at least he will be off the streets. Be careful he might escape, I literally had to drag him here. He does not want to go on with life. He wants god to open the pearly gates to let him enter into heaven to be with his wife."

After a week in the hospital, Henry was feeling better, stronger. He was now breathing on his own. He gained a few pounds. There is a saying that hospital food is terrible not for Henry, he was chowing down his meals as if he knew it was his last meal."

To no one's knowledge Henry was regaining his strength to escape from the hospital. All nonperishable food, Henry was using a pillow case to hide the food. He was planning on sneaking out during the day when the hospital is the busiest.

A few more days, he will be ready to escape from the hospital. When the time came to leave the hospital, Henry retrieved the clothes Larry gave him, it's a good thing that Henry kept the clothes in a small pouch attached to his waist. He ran to a nearby washroom changed into his clothes and out the door. Henry made it to the elevator without being detected. He hurried out the door unnoticed.

Henry waited for nightfall to go retrieve his belongings in the shed. He did a quick search for tiny, could not find him. Henry was quiet as a mouse, picked up his stuff, hurried back to the main road, only to disappear between buildings. Larry never seen or heard of Henry again.

It was already too late when one of the nurse's discovered Henry was not in his bed. They did a thorough search on every floor, all around the hospital, the parking lot, asked the people, outside the hospital if they had seen Henry outside. Every answer was negative.

Henry was no longer on the premises. Larry received a call from the hospital that Henry escaped, and they could not find him. Larry said, if Henry showed up at his place, he will notify them.

When Larry hung up the phone, he ran to the shed. He was too late. The shed was empty. Larry was upset, but there was nothing he could do. The one good thing that really helped Henry there was no known photographs of him anywhere. He could roam the streets with no worry someone would recognize him. Only a handful of people knew him.

He was now across town, away from everybody that would be able to find him. Finding him was like trying to find a needle in a haystack. After a few days Henry was feeling sick again. He did not leave his makeshift shack for several days. He spent most days sleeping. His final demise was fast approaching.

CHAPTER 14

Back in South Africa, a young woman was thinking about her little brother she left behind in the United States so many years ago. She was now clean, sober and drug free. She started a new job; her goal was to save enough money to go back to the states and try to find her brother. She was aware it would not be an easy task. Patience, hard work was the key to get results.

Meanwhile back in the states Henry was really struggling. He was able to find a homeless shelter that took him in. It was only for a short period of time. The shelters where lacking donations, beds, in order for every homeless person to have a chance to enjoy a warm bed and hot meals for at least ten days, a rotation needed to be done.

After ten days Henry was back on the street panhandling. While at the shelter, Henry was given some medication for his cold. He was feeling a little better but not a one hundred percent. Another homeless man took over is shack while he was at the shelter. Henry found some cardboard, an old canvas in a trash can, a few boards. Henry put his makeshift shack together a block away from his previous location.

Every day he wondered when God will be coming to take him away. Henry was aware if he committed suicide, it was like murder. Even if it's your own life, the life does not belong to you it belongs to the giver of life, and he does not appreciate life being destroyed by suicide. If there is a chance that you do not go to heaven when taking your own life Henry wanted no part of it.

He will wait until the doors of heaven are open for him and Kaccha waiting for him at the doors. Every night before falling asleep, he imagined himself floating to the gates of heaven with Kaccha waiting for him with a great big smile, arms wide open. He could not wait to see her again.

The amount of money, Louane was putting away to go to the states was increasing every week, seventy percent of her paycheck was going into her bank account. She started to put a plan together for when she arrives in the states, her first stop will be the town where she was living before the tragic car accident that took the lives of her mother and father.

She was anxious to get going and be reunited with her little brother. Also, on her mind would Henry be happy to see her or having nothing to do with her for leaving him behind? Every evening back in his shack, Henry would say.

" One more day gone, one less day to wait to join Kaccha."

Henry made friends with a few men in the same predicament he was in. They would exchange stories on how they ended up living on the streets. Some were drunks, drug addicts, war veterans, after putting their lives on the line for their country, their only reward was panhandling to survive. Henry could feel the bitterness in their voices.

One morning Henry and his friends were told by the cops there was a new bylaw prohibiting to panhandle on city streets, one of the men challenged, dared the police to chase him off the streets. He was previously involved in a few fights with the cops. The man was an Iraq war veteran, he always carried on him, his service revolver.

He once told his friends, he came up with an eighty cents solution to deal with the pesky cops, the price of a bullet. One afternoon he was shot dead in the middle of the street while brandishing the revolver in front of the cops. He refused to put the gun down. When he aimed his gun in the direction of the police officers, they opened fire. He was dead before hitting the ground.

Henry noticed; it was becoming more violent. One man shot dead by the cops. A day later one homeless man stabbed and killed by a newcomer on the streets. The man walked away with a few dollars from the victim's pocket and the meager belongings of the man he just killed.

The police did a small investigation. The police department did not want to waste their time and effort, especially valuable manpower for a hobo living on the streets. They had bigger fish to fry. The cops took a few notes, a few pictures, talked to a few witnesses, that was basically it for the investigation, the cops did not come back for a follow up or even search the neighborhood for suspects.

The way the investigation was conducted, the police department was acting as if the killer did the victim a favor by killing him to end his miserable life, for the cops one less street bum to worry about.

The cops spent more time hassling the homeless to move to another part of town than they did on the murder investigation. Homeless people were a thorn in their side. They were considered a waste of time and money. After the stabbing Henry packed his stuff, moved five blocks away. The first couple of nights Henry slept in between buildings with no cover from the elements.

The third day at his new location, he was chased away. The homeless man panhandling that section of town did not want any newcomers. One more individual panhandling would reduce the amount of money tossed in his can. Henry made is way to a side street with less traffic to avoid any future conflicts with the other panhandlers.

He found a spot, again he gathered enough stuff to build himself a small shelter made of cardboard, a few pieces of broken lumber and some plastic, all the items were retrieved from garbage bins. Henry noticed he was the only homeless person in his new surroundings this could be good or bad. He would be alone for panhandling, or they did not want any of his kind in the area.

He will soon know, hopefully it will be his new home or will get chased away by the residents. After a few days passersby started to put money in his can, at last a sweet victory for him. Louane was getting ready to go to the states to find her brother, her passport was in order, two more paychecks to go, she purchased her plane ticket, Louane was raring to go.

Some of her coworkers wished her luck, some said she was crazy to go on such a quest. One of her coworkers who was a close friend kept reminding her,

" This is foolish. A waste of time and money if you ask me. What makes you think he is still in America? You know he could be anywhere in the world. "

" I am very well aware of that but it's something I need to do. When he was adopted by the parents of a friend, he wanted me to go with him. I said no, I stayed put where I was, I started using drugs, you know hang out with the wrong crowd. I left the United States to come back home, I did not even try to find him to say goodbye. For me it is an unfinished chapter in my life that I need to complete."

" Are you planning on coming back?"

" It all depends."

" Depends on what?"

" I do not know yet, I guess I will find out when I get there. Anymore comments or questions? I know that you really do not want me to go. Please understand he is my only brother, I have to repair the wrong I did to him, hopefully he will forgive me."

Since Kaccha passed away, Henry was missing his sister even more. Every day he would wonder where she was, what she was doing, was she happy. Was he an uncle? Living on the street like him, and not in very good health.

The chances of ever seeing his sister again where next to none. What a nosedive his life as taken. Happy one day, good job, good home, married to the woman of his dreams. In a matter of seconds when Kaccha tripped down the stairs it all came tumbling down like a house of cards

" Look at me today. I keep asking the same question over and over I must have done terrible things in my previous life to have such a debt to pay but why punish Kaccha? I do not understand why my life crashed and burned in the prime of our lives. I lost everything and everybody, I loved and cared for, my sister who left me behind, Mr. Moore passed away, Mrs. Moore never loved me, poor Lucas is now mentally unstable because of two tours of duty in Afghanistan. I barely know my two step sisters. I hope I have paid my dues and my next life will be less stressful."

Finally, Louane was on her way to the airport. She was really determined to find Henry. To do so she gave up a comfortable life, friends, she quit her job. She was anxious, nervous but confident her trip was not all for nothing, she will not stop searching until she finds her brother.

She said goodbye to her friends who drove her to the airport, she boarded the plane with great anticipation, relieved she was finally on the plane. She said out loud.

" I am on my way little brother, cannot wait to see you."

Some of the passengers were looking at her, she apologized for talking out loud, she took her seat next to a middle-aged woman named Leslie. She introduced herself to Louane.

" We will be shoulder to shoulder for hours, might as well introduce myself my name is Leslie. I am happy to make your acquaintance."

Louane was happy to have a friendly passenger sitting next to her and especially someone from South Africa. A real bonus for her.

" Likewise, from what part of South Africa are you from? I live in east London a town called Brookville."

Leslie was surprised she would meet a fellow passenger close to her home.

" Really, I live in Greenfields, only a short distance away if you take the road r.72. It's a twenty-minute drive from Brookville. My daughter Emma has been living in the states for three years now, with her American husband. I am on my way to visit her for the first time since she moved. They met on the internet of all places. The internet can you believe that?"

" Yes, I do, I call it cyber love, everything is smooth and dandy until they meet in person. I always said, love is great until your first fight."

" When her husband Thomas flew over to see her. They had their fair share of ups and downs, but they were able to work it out. Emma is expecting their first child, a boy, my first grandson."

They talked nonstop until the plane landed in Sacramento, they said their goodbyes.

" Well, lots of luck finding your brother, I hope you do, family is very important in life. It was a pleasure meeting and talking to you, if you are ever in Greenfields stop for a cup of tea."

" I will, have a nice visit with you daughter and her husband. Congratulations on being a future grandmother, goodbye."

Now in the states Louane was eager to get the ball rolling and find her brother. She picked up her rental car at the airport and was on her way to the house of the folks who adopted Henry. Mr. and Mrs. Moore's house. She could not get there soon enough, hoping the Moore family was still living in the house.

Henry was dealing with a cough and a fever. With the money he collected he was able to buy a bottle of pills and a bottle of cough syrup. He was hoping they would both do the job, bring down the fever, stop the coughing. The next day Henry was feeling better, he was at his usual spot to collect a little bit of money to be able to eat. The cost of the medicine took all of his money except for a few dollars.

One day Henry noticed right across the street from him. A homeless man was panhandling. He was thinking there goes the neighborhood.

One beggar across the street from me, really, he has a lot of nerve I am sure he could have found another place instead of invading my space. Henry could barely survive as it was, now his slim pickings will be cut in half because of the intruder across the street. Henry had the urge to go across the street to talk to him.

After a few days, Henry was surprised to see the new tenant across the street coming towards him.

" Hi, my name is Willy, I hope you do not mind my presence across the street?"

" Henry"

" Come again."

" My name is Henry."

" Hi Henry.

The reason I wanted to talk to you if you would be interested in a partnership with me. A 50/50 deal?"

" I don't think so."

" Why not?"

" First of all, you are invading my space, this street is two miles long. Do not tell me you could not find a comfortable place for you to panhandle instead of right across the street from me. What is the matter with you?"

" I am not invading your space, you do not own the sidewalks, for your information there is nothing wrong with me. My purpose for me to be across the street was to form a friendship with you and be partners. It would be a win, win situation for the both of us. We could keep each other company, no more lonely nights for the both of us."

" Why would I do that? I don't know you, you don't know me, what makes you think I can trust you or you trusting me? Go back where you came from and leave me alone."

" You don't have a to be jerk with me, I only wanted to know if you would be interested in a partnership that's all, if you do not ask you do not know right it was not my intention to offend you, I am sorry."

" I am sorry Willy; I did not mean to be a jerk. You can stay here; I will get my things and move somewhere else."

" You stay Henry, I will get out of your way first thing in the morning."

" It's ok, I was thinking of going back to my old stomping grounds. I kept on putting it off, now I have a reason to go back."

" Ok then good luck."

They shook hands Willy made his way back across the street, the next morning Henry gathered his things. He waved to Willy and began is journey back to his old neighborhood where he was living with the love of his life. In his mind that is where he belongs.

CHAPTER 15

It took Henry several days to reach his destination. He stopped a few minutes in front of his house. Tears were flowing down his cheeks. We were so happy, full of life, a bright, joyful future ahead of us. We were going to grow old together in this house, our home but everything was taken away from us. I wish the new owners of our little paradise a long and healthy, accident-free life.

Because of the bank repossessing the house. The new owners were able to buy the house dirt cheap. Financial institutions do not like and try to avoid is having an empty house or building on their hands that will eventually cost the financial institutions money to upkeep the place.

Louane walked over to the house where the Moore family used to live. Rang the doorbell. When a young man answered the door.

" Do you live here."

" Yes."

" Is your mother or daddy home?"

" Mom the lady at the door wants to talk to you."

" Hi, my name is Louane, I am looking for the previous owners of the house."

" Do you mean Arnold and Doreen Stevenson?"

" Who?"

" The Stevenson's, we bought the house a year ago. The Stevenson's are the ones who sold us the house."

" I am looking for the previous owners, Mr. and Mrs. Moore. The Stevenson's purchase the house from."

" Sorry the family name does not ring a bell. The only thing I know, is when we purchased the house, Mr. Stevenson said we were the fourth owners of the house."

" I am sorry to have bothered you, when my little brother was adopted by Mr. and Mrs. Moore this is where they lived at the time. I was a rebel I did not want to move. I remained with the foster family I has living with at the time. and I eventually moved back to my home country in South Africa."

" That's where the accent comes from. The only thing I can do for you is give you the phone number to reach Mr. or Mrs. Stevenson. They gave us their number in case we needed to get in touch with them."

" That would be great."

" Come in for a minute, while I get the number for you."

The lady looked in her purse, found her little notebook, wrote the phone number on a small piece of paper, and handed the piece of paper to Louane.

" Thank you, your very kind, you do not know how much I appreciate this, thank you very much."

" You're welcome, I hope you do find your brother, good luck. "

Louane stepped out of the house disappointed, she knew there would be setbacks. She was optimistic with good detective work; she will find her brother. The phone number in her hands was a good start.

Before checking in a hotel for the night, she drove in front of the house that used to be her home with mom, dad, and little brother Henry so many years ago. She was able to find a very nice and clean room that was not too pricey, before going to bed although small she was happy with the progress, she made on her first day of searching.

" Tomorrow is another day, I hope I can take another step forward towards finding Henry. First thing in the morning I will start my day with a phone call hoping it will lead me somewhere."

First thing the next morning, Louane noticed it was a local number, the Stevenson's should not be very hard to find. She dialed the number, no answer, the answering machine came on, this was her message.

" Hi, my name is Louane, I was given your number from the lady who bought your house a year ago. The reason I am calling if you have any knowledge of where Mr. and Mrs. Moore moved or their phone number, can you please call me at 881-555-0034 please."

Louane went back to her room hoping to hear from Mr. or Mrs. Stevenson, she waited all day, no callbacks. She tried again the next morning, again the answering machine. She left another detailed message. She waited all day again no callback.

She tried again the next morning to reach Mr. or Mrs. Stevenson. No answer, but this time Louane put an urgency to her message, hoping it was enough for prompting a callback by someone. Around four o'clock in the afternoon her phone rang, she ran across the room to answer the phone, unfortunately it was a wrong number. Again, still no callback.

Waiting for a callback that might not materialize, the next morning she took a different approach. She did a search with the phone number; she was able to find the address of the residence of Mr. and Mrs. Stevenson. She said to herself.

" Why did I not think about that in the first place. I would have saved a lot of time and frustration waiting for a call. I need to hurry and move my ass and make up for the time I have lost. "

She drove to the address, waited until a car pulled up in the driveway. A woman got out of the car; Louane rushed to go talk to her.

" I am sorry to bother you, my name is Louane, I am the one who keeps leaving a message on your answering machine for the past couple of days. "

The woman looked at her and said.

" Since my husband left me for another woman, the woman who he left me for keeps on calling and leaving nasty messages on my answering machine, I do not even bother to listen to the messages, when I see there is a message, I hit the delete button."

" That's why I was not getting a callback."

" Please come in my name is Lorna."

" Hi Lorna, a pleasure to meet you, my name is Louane."

" Would you like a cup of coffee."

" Yes, please I would love one."

Both ladies sat at the dinner table drinking coffee, Louane explained to Lorna why she was leaving phone messages. Lorna apologized for not listening to her messages. Louane and Lorna hit it right off the bat they became friends.

Lorna provided Louane with the address of Mr. and Mrs. Moore and their phone number. She advised Louane it was a long time ago when her and her ex-husband purchased the Moore house, the phone number or address might not be valid anymore. The two ladies talked well into the early morning hours. When Louane noticed the time, she got up from the couch.

" Wow look at the time, I apologize for overstaying my welcome. I am so sorry."

" No not at all, I enjoy your company it's been some time since I had a good chat with someone. Do you have a place to stay tonight?"

" Not yet I will look for a motel near here."

" Nonsense, I have a spare bedroom that you can use."

" Are you sure? I do not want to be a bother."

" No bother at all, I am the one offering you a place to sleep tonight."

" Ok I accept your invitation, you're too kind."

Henry found a little cozy spot down the street, he settled in for the night, the next morning Henry was again looking for some material in order for him to build a small shelter, again he was able to find pieces of wood an old boat cover and carboard boxes.

When Henry was done putting up is new home, he looked across the street. He noticed a old lazy boy chair at the curb ready to be picked up by the garbage man. Henry raced across the street and dragged the chair into what he now called his new place the den. The chair was broken and torn but Henry was estatic, boy oh boy what a find.

The next day Henry dragged the chair in the entrance of his so-called den, where he will be sitting from now on to panhandle for money. Although old and turned, the chair was a lot more comfortable than sitting on cement. Everyday Henry would sit in the chair.

At night push the chair back in his little den in case someone might want to steal his luxury chair. His health was starting to go downhill again. Fever, coughing, aching bones. Henry took the few remaining pain relief pills from the bottle, gulped down the remaining cough syrup in the bottle.

The next morning Henry was feeling a little better but by the end of the day his cough intensified. He could not sleep because of the constant coughing.

The next afternoon Henry fell asleep for a few minutes in his chair a couple of kids stole his money, when he woke up, he noticed his can was empty. He was to use the money to go buy a bottle of pain relievers and some cough sirop. He will have to wait until tomorrow to get some medicine.

The next day, Henry was dead tired, unable to sleep for two nights, the lack of sleep was taking its toll. Henry collapsed in his chair, coughing like his lungs were ready to explode, he was now too weak to get up from the chair.

From a lack of sleep and food Henry lost consciousness. Every two- or three-hours Henry would regain consciousness for a few minutes and again lose consciousness. Henry was slowly dying in his chair, pedestrians walked by not paying any attention to Henry.

The next morning Lorna and Louane went out for breakfast, after returning home, Louane dialed the phone number Lorna gave her. A man answered the phone, he told Louane she had the wrong number,

" Sir do you reside at the address 3489 Richard Street in Chicago?"

" No, I do not, who is this, who am I talking too?"

" I am sorry sir; I have the wrong number and the wrong address."

Louane was not surprised after so many years it would have been pure luck if Mr. or Mrs. Moore would have answered the phone. Louane called the airline booked a ticket for Chicago. Her flight was for ten pm that night. Louane spent the day with her new friend Lorna.

When Louane left for the airport, she promised Lorna she would stay in touch. At the airport Louane returned her rental car and booked a rental car at the Chicago O'Hare airport. At ten pm Louane was on her way to Chicago. After a smooth flight, Louane landed in Chicago, picked up her rental car, booked a room at a nearby hotel, where she would spend a good portion of the day sleeping.

The next morning after breakfast, she was on her way to 3489 Richard Street, her heart was beating twice as fast, when she turned the corner on Richard Street and saw the house only a few hundred feet away.

In the meantime, a pedestrian who walked back and forth every day to go to work noticed Henry was still in his chair and had not moved for a couple of days. He walked over to Henry and immediately called 911.

Henry was rushed to the hospital by ambulance in critical condition, Henry was severely dehydrated, a very weak pulse, still unconscious when the ambulance reached the hospital, the emergency room doctor was able to stabilize him and transferred him to the intensive care unit.

After several days Henry woke up, he immediately recognized the place. It was the same hospital who took care of Kaccha. The memories came flooding back. He spent a few more days in the intensive care unit then by coincidence was moved to the same floor where Kaccha took her final breath.

Louane parked her car in front of the house, walked over, rang the doorbell, no answer, she rang the doorbell again, still no answer. She realized it was Saturday, they might be gone for the weekend. As she was walking back to her car, a neighbor who was trimming her rose bushes, came over to talk to her.

" Hi, are you looking for Martha and Matt? They are gone for the weekend, they will not be back until tomorrow, they went camping with the kids."

" Hi, I was looking for Mr. and Mrs. Moore."

" You're not from the area am I right?"

" Yes."

" That's what I figured, when you mentioned Mr. and Mrs. Moore, when Mr. Moore died, Mrs. Moore sold the house, she moved along with her son who was in the army to a place called Long Grove. That was a few years ago."

" Mr. Moore is deceased and Lucas was in the army. "

" Very nice people, but when Lucas came back from a second tour in Afghanistan, he was never the same. We now call Martha and Matt. The M&M's couple."

" Thank you very much for the information you have been very helpful. Thank you so much."

" If you do not mind my asking, are you a relative?"

" Yes and no, you see when my parents died in a car accident, Henry my brother was adopted by the Moore family, I went back to South Africa, I lost track of my little brother, I am trying to find him."

" Boy that's quite the challenge, it's like teaching a deaf mute how to talk. How long have you been in the states looking for your brother?"

" About a week now."

" Well good for you, you made good progress in a very short period of time, I do hope you find your little brother alive and well,"

" Again, thank you, I really appreciate it. God bless."

" You too. Goodbye now."

" Goodbye."

Louane was happy she was making headway in her search to find Henry. It was now one pm. She went back to her motel to spend the night and relax and drive to Long Grove in the morning.

She entered the coordinates in her cellphone. She was not able to find a phone number for Mrs. Moore. Hopefully Mrs. Moore did not decide to move again. Mrs. Moore's phone number was probably unlisted. In a town the size of Long Grove with a population of eight thousand someone is bound to know Mrs. Moore.

The next morning Lounne was out of bed at seven am. Eager to hit the road to take another step forward to accomplish her mission to find her little brother. After a small breakfast she hit the road, destination Long Grove.

As for Henry he was now alert, but still very sick. Doctor Applebee recognized Henry, so did the nurses. With an oxygen mask helping him breathe he was unable to talk. He gave them a thumbs up. Henry was now stable but still fragile. The doctor joked with Henry.

" You have made some progress my dear friend but not yet enough for you to go dancing."

The nurses each took their turns to go check on their old friend. Unfortunately, Henry would not recover from his illness. Henry would never utter a word again. The end of his days among the living was near. When Louane arrived in Long Grove, right away she started asking questions to some of the town's residents. She did not have any luck the first day.

The following day, she purchased poster size paper, black markers and pins. She wrote on the posters, if anyone knew Mrs. Moore or her son Lucas, to please call her cell phone. She also wrote it was essential and very important for her to locate Mrs. Moore or her son.

She pinned a poster on billboards of every business in town. She also kept the momentum with her search to find Mrs. Moore. She quickly found out there where several Moore families living in town. She also contacted the local radio station to broadcast her message.

A lot of dead ends, she did not despair, she was optimistic she would get a major break in her search for Henry. That night she went to bed with a hunch that tomorrow her phone will ring with Mrs. Moore at the other end of the line.

The phone call she was waiting for did not materialize for a couple of days. Finally, one afternoon, her phone rang and lo and behold, Mrs. Moore was at the end of the line.

" Hello."

" Yes, Louane, I understand you are looking for me, this is Mrs. Moore."

" Thank you so much for calling, you cannot know how this phone call means to me."

" What can I do for you?"

" I am trying to find Henry; would you know is whereabouts?"

" Well my dear, would you like to come over for a cup of coffee?"

" Yes, that would be super."

Mrs. Moore provided Louane with driving instructions to get to her house. She was only five minutes away. She jumped in her car. She could hardly contain her excitement.

In the meantime, back at the hospital Henry was slowly slipping away to meet the grim reaper. The doctor was worried about Henry's vital signs. He knew Henry was fighting a losing battle. His immune system was too weak to fight infections.

Henry was exposed to the elements for a long period of time, recurring pneumonia did a lot of damage to his lungs, some bacteria in his blood. The odds for a recovery where next to none. It would take a miracle for Henry to pull through. The only thing the doctor could do was to keep him comfortable. Henry motioned with his hands that he would be soon going to the big house in heaven.

When Louane arrived at Mrs. Moore's house, she got out of her car, ran to the front door. Lucas opened the door.

" Louane is that you?"

" Yes, Lucas it's me."

" You have grown up since the last time I saw you, you turned out to be a very beautiful woman."

" Thank you you're not so bad yourself."

Mrs. Moore greeted her with a big smile and a hug. Over coffee she told Louane Henry's story. When finished Mrs. Moore admitted to Louane the last time she talked to Henry she was not very nice to him. She was mad when she said the things she said. She could not help but feel remorse for everything she said.

Louane was really sad. She missed the wedding of her little brother; she never met her sister in-law. Louane spent the remainder of the day with Mrs. Moore and Lucas.

Lucas talked about his career in the army. The men in his platoon he had no choice to leave behind and so forth. He also talked about his stay at a mental institution. The medication he needs to take every day to help him cope. All day Louane and Lucas were hitting on each other. They both could feel the attraction between the two.

" I cannot believe how beautiful you are Louane absolutely gorgeous."

" Thanks, like I said, your quite handsome yourself."

Mrs. Moore knew where that was going. The two really digged each other. Louane booked a flight for two to sand Diego, Lucas wanted to tag along. Mrs. Moore was a little hesitant for him to travel.

" Do not worry mom, Louane will take good care of me. I will go pack our flight is for tomorrow morning. Louane you are not going anywhere tonight; the sofa is yours." when everyone turned in for the evening.

Louane could hear Lucas battling his demons in his sleep. Lucas was back on the battlefield in Afghanistan.

The next morning Louane and Lucas were on a plane bound for San Diego. Louane did not say a word about Lucas talking in his sleep and still fighting the war in Afghanistan. Lucas talked about Henry, his life, profession, and the accident that changed Henry's life as being one of the happiest men on earth and to be the saddest man on earth.

Kaccha was his life. When Kaccha tumbled down the stairs Henry's life also tumbled, he was never able to get back up. After renting like Lucas said wheels at the airport, they made their way to the San Diego general hospital. Once at the hospital both Lucas and Louane were deeply saddened about the news of Kaccha's passing, and Henry barely clinging on to life.

The doctor met Lucas and Louane at the elevator. Lucas shook hands with the doctor.

" Nice to see you again Lucas."

" Likewise. We came here to get some news about Kaccha."

When Dr. Applebee told them Kaccha was gone and Henry is barely clinging on to life, boy talk about a double wammy.

" Nice to finally meet you Louane, Henry talked about his big sister all the time, my name is Doctor Applebee. I was the doctor that took care of Kaccha in her final days. A warning for both of you, Henry will not recover from his illness his immune system is too weak to battle infections. It is only a matter of hours before Henry leaves us for good. Follow me."

When Louane saw Henry, all grown up, lying on his death bed, she could not hold back her tears, Lucas embraced her in his arms. Henry's eyes where barely open when he spotted Lucas, you could see the joy in Henry's face. Lucas went over, kissed Henry on the forehead. Henry could not keep his eyes of Lucas.

" Henry, I have someone very special with me today, your sister Louane."

Louane approached the bed, Henry was crying, everybody in the room including the doctor was crying. She gave Henry a hug and kept both his hands in her hands.

" I do not know if they told you, Henry was in South Africa looking for you when Kaccha fell down the stairs."

Through her tears, she said.

" He came looking for me."

Louane looked at Lucas.

" Yes, it's true he went looking for you."

Louane and Lucas each held a hand of their little brother.

" We are not going anywhere little buddy."

" Like Lucas said we are not going anywhere."

The doctor advised the hospital staff, Lucas and Louane were staying put and to bring them some chairs. The nurse who took care of Kaccha and now Henry only had praise for Henry. They both kept their hands clamped in Henry's hands. After a long evening they both fell asleep.

To everyone's surprise Henry lasted another day, always keeping his eyes on Louane and Lucas. They could see in his eyes how happy he was to see Lucas and especially Louane, in the evening Henry closed his eyes. Louane and Lucas settled in for the night, holding Henry's hands.

Louane and Lucas woke up to the sound of Henry crying and talking. His eyes were wide open he closed his eyes one last time, he was ready to go with having his sister and brother by his side. He was not going to die alone. With his eyes closed, Henry was talking his voice was too weak to understand to whom Henry was talking too. Louane put her ear one inch from his mouth she was able to hear is final words.

" Kaccha my love, Lucas and Louane my precious sister are with me. I am not alone anymore, I am making my way to you, please open the doors of heaven for me so we can be together for eternity, there you are, you look so beautiful all dressed in white. "

He took a few long breaths, and he was gone. Henry could see Kaccha in the middle of a glowing light dressed in white, arms extended waiting for him. He was at peace; his mom and dad were also waiting for him.

" I am here mom and dad."

They needed to sedate Louane she was losing control of her emotions. Lucas remained composed to be strong for Louane.

" No, no, no please Henry come back, I just got here. Please don't go please. There was so much I wanted to talk to you about. Oh my god no, bring him back, please bring him back, I will never ask you for another favor ever again, please just this once pleaaaaaaase, I beg you, please, Henry, I love you, I am so sorry for leaving you behind. I love you my little brother. Oh god no he cannot be gone. It's a mistake doctor, check him again."

With the help of the medication Louane was able to calm down. She fell asleep in a chair beside the bed. Dr Applebee was crying, the nurses were crying, they each took their time to say goodbye to the sweetest man they ever met. Dr Applebee said a few words.

" We will let her sleep for a little while, when she wakes up, she can go down to the morgue and say her final goodbyes."

" Can you leave Henry here until she wakes up? "

" I am sorry I cannot do that; they will be taking his body to the morgue in a few minutes. We try to avoid keeping the deceased in the room.

The patients do not need to see the body with a sheet over his or her head. That's the worst thing for a patient to see. Some start thinking, they might be next."

" I understand doctor thank you."

" Here they come."

Lucas took a last look at Henry.

" I will see you up there my little buddy, in the meantime take good care of Kaccha."

" You know Lucas like they say father like son for Louane and Henry it is brother like sister. She reacted the same way and said the exact words Henry said when Kaccha passed away."

Henry's personal things were put in a bag and given to Lucas. They took Henry down to the morgue, Lucas watched them walk away, until they reached the elevator. He wiped his tears, waited for Louane to wake up. After a half hour of sleep, Louane woke up.

" Lucas where is Henry, what did they do with him?"

" They brought him down to the morgue."

" And you let them do that."

" There was nothing I could do."

" Your right, I am sorry, I am overwhelmed, I cannot believe he is gone. I just got here. I wish I could have been able to spend more time with him."

" Yes, I know, the problem is death waits for no one. If you want to say your final goodbyes we can go down to the morgue."

" No, I would rather not, I won't be able to control my emotions and again make a fool of myself. I cannot bare the thought to see Henry lying on a table among other dead people and people crying for their loved one."

The next day Louane made funeral arrangements, Henry would be cremated, the funeral was scheduled for the end of the week. In the meantime, Mrs. Moore flew in from Long Grove. Louane and Lucas picked her up at the airport. She hugged Louane.

" I am so sorry for your lost, last time I spoke to Henry, I was angry with him, I told him terrible things, he died with all those nasty words in his head. I apologize for being so rude to Henry. Can you forgive me I will never get the chance to tell him how sorry I am. He was alone, he reached out to me, and I let him down. "

" Thank you, Mrs. Moore, there's nothing to forgive. But for me I will live with guilt and regrets for the rest of my life."

" Mom did you have any idea how much Henry loved you? He adored you. He was so proud having you as a mother. I never heard him say anything negative of you. You were his rock. "

" I will feel remorse and guilt for the rest of my days. The things I told him; he never said a word back to me."

" Mom the funeral is on Friday, two days from now, let's get you settled in and grab something to eat."

" May I ask who is paying for the funeral?

" I am Mrs. Moore."

" Keep your money Louane I will pay for Henry's funeral it's the least I can do for him."

Like Kaccha's funeral, there was only a small gathering of a few friends from the hospital and Henry's stepsisters. what Louane had to say, brought everyone to tears.

" My dear little brother, I am so sorry for abandoning you when we were kids, I left the country without knowing how you were. Knowing you came to South Africa to find me, is tearing my heart apart. I should have been there for you, but no I was selfish only thinking about myself, in your time of need, you were all alone. I love you more now than ever. I did not have the opportunity to make amends for all the pain and anguish that I caused you. Rest in peace, be happy with your wife in heaven."

Lucas also said a few words.

" Little brother, my best buddy, I am also guilty of leaving you all alone, I went away to fight someone else's war. I camc back emotionally scarred for the rest of my days. Yes, I lost friends and had no choice to leave my fallen men on the battlefield, but it does not compare for the way I feel today. You were a better soldier, a better warrior than I was. You started fighting in grade school until you closed your eyes for the last time. That's what we call a true warrior a true hero. You knew that every day you were fighting a losing battle, but no matter what, you got up every morning and went to war. Your body was never big enough to carry that big heart of yours. Rest in peace my little buddy and say hi to Kaccha for me."

Mrs. Moore also wanted to say a few words.

" My dear Henry, I hope if you are listening, please forgive me for what I said to you the last time we spoke. I never told you this, but I was very proud of you. You became a fine young, devoted man with a big heart too big for your chest. Rest in peace my dear son, you deserve it. Your battles are now over."

Nurse Gloria wanted to say a few words.

" Henry at the hospital we got to know, believe me when I say this, you were a inspiration for all of us. The love and devotion for your wife was incredible, never seen before and you became part of our family. We all love you and we will miss you. Rest in peace my dear friend. You are now an angel in heaven. You were a real teacher who taught us what life, love and devotion really is."

When the funeral was over, Mrs. Moore, Lucas and Louane made their way back to the motel.

" Now that all of this is over, what are you planning on doing?"

" Well Mrs. Moore, I think a will stay for a little while longer."

Louane reached for Lucas, he took her in his arms and kissed her.

" You know Louane I am damaged goods and I do not know what the future holds for me. "

I don't care, we will be together that's all that matters. "

" All righty then, you two love birds coming home soon?"

Louane took the bag with Henry's personal stuff. She was looking for stuff she wanted to keep as a momento of her little brother when she spotted a piece of paper in the back pocket of Henry's pants. She unfolded the piece of paper and burst out crying. She said.

" Mrs. Moore, Lucas you need to hear what is written on this piece of paper."

With tears in her eyes, she read the content of the letter.

I hope my letter finds its way to one of my family members. Louane my dearest sister, how I longed to know if you were ok, enjoying a good life. Not knowing was eating me inside. You did not get to know Kaccha, on our wedding day, I closed my eyes and wished that you were by my side. I guess I will never know if I am an uncle. I forgive you for leaving me behind. It is ok. How can I not forgive you, my sister that I love with all my heart. You did not get to know Kaccha, the only way that I can describe her. She was an angel sent from heaven. Only if it was only for a short while, I cherished every moment with her. I have accepted and forgiven God for taking her away from me.

Lucas, my rock my best buddy in the whole world. When you went to war, I was there with you, I could not let you go alone. That day in the schoolyard was one of the best days in my life. It brought me to you. In my heart I said thank you to the bullies for bringing you into my life. No bullies, no Lucas. I was devastated when I heard about your situation. I will always look up to you no matter what, you are my hero.

Dad you will never know how grateful I am for accepting me in your family. You are the best of men in the whole wide world. Mrs. Moore, I am so sorry to be a disappointment for you. Please know that I will always love you. You mean the world to me. I hope that someday you will find it in your heart to forgive me. Kaccha was the love of my life, and I could not leave her side. My two adoring stepsisters, you accepted me in your family, and I will always be grateful. Love you always. "

Henry

Wow what a letter, I will make copies of the letter so that you each have one."

" Good idea Louane."

" Thank you, Lucas."

" Mom our flight is for tomorrow night; do you want to tag along?"

" Might as well, I have nothing else to do."

After only six months together Louane and Lucas tied the knot, Louane never went back to South Africa. They named their first son Henry.

The end.

Summary

A man that kept is word to his wife. He never abandoned Kaccha no matter the cost. His promise ruined and cost him his life, but Henry would not have it any other way. His love for Kaccha was so strong and deep he did not care about himself only Kaccha's wellbeing after her accident. He was a true warrior, every day in a constant battle to keep Kaccha by his side. Alone in this big world of ours Henry kept on fighting a losing battle. This book is fictional, but could we do and endure what Henry did for his wife? That's a question that is very hard to answer.

www.ingramcontent.com/pod-product-compliance
Lightning Source LLC
Chambersburg PA
CBHW070658010826
48975CB00014B/2219